His Current Woman

His Current Woman

Jerzy Pilch

Translated from the Polish by Bill Johnston

Hydra Books/Northwestern University Press
EVANSTON, ILLINOIS

Hydra Books
Northwestern University Press
Evanston, Illinois 60208-4210

Originally published in Polish in 1995 as *Inne rozkosze*. Copyright © 1995 by
Jerzy Pilch. English translation copyright © 2002 by Northwestern University
Press. Published 2002. All rights reserved.

Printed in the United States of America

10 9 8 7 6 5 4 3 2 1

ISBN 0-8101-1918-8

Library of Congress Cataloging-in-Publication Data

Pilch, Jerzy, 1952–
[Inne rozkosze. English]
His current woman / Jerzy Pilch ; translated from the Polish by Bill Johnston.
p. cm.
"Hydra books."
ISBN 0-8101-1918-8
I. Johnston, Bill. II. Title.
PG7175.I49 I5613 2002
891.8'538—dc21
2001006877

The paper used in this publication meets the minimum requirements of the
American National Standard for Information Sciences—Permanence of Paper for
Printed Library Materials, ANSI Z39.48-1984.

Publikacja finansowana przez Instytut Adama Mickiewicza–
Polski Fundusz Literatury.
[This publication is financed by the Adam Mickiewicz Institute–
Polish Literary Fund.]

©POLAND

His Current Woman

1

When in the year of our Lord 1990 Paweł Kohoutek, Doctor of Veterinary Medicine, looked out of the window and beheld his current woman crossing the lawn, with his usual conceited fatalism he imagined that an adventure had befallen him which ought to serve as a warning for all. Kohoutek's current woman was wearing a navy-blue overcoat; her divine skull was covered with a funky little hat, while the colossal suitcase she was dragging behind her left a dark trail of final defeat in the pale November grass.

Even if she had just dropped by to chat with me, even if she were merely popping in casually and unexpectedly, that alone would be a sufficiently terrifying story, thought Kohoutek. That alone would be a story worthy of a book. But Kohoutek's current woman hadn't just come by to visit. She was hauling the suitcase along with both hands, while upon her narrow shoulders she bore a backpack filled to bursting. Though Kohoutek had known her for a mere seventeen weeks, he knew perfectly well what was in the suitcase and what was in the backpack. In the suitcase were books, and in the backpack all of her other possessions. Kohoutek could close his eyes and list the items one by one, with the greatest of ease naming all the components of her wardrobe: seven black T-shirts, two white blouses, two khaki men's shirts, one gray sweat suit with white trim, three black miniskirts, one pair of jeans, two pairs of low-heeled slip-on shoes, a pair of thigh-length boots which had belonged to Kohoutek's current woman's mother, a black turtleneck sweater, a man's gray tweed jacket in which she looked fabulous, panty hose, and several dozen pairs of exclusively white panties in various styles. Yes, Kohoutek's current woman had packed up all her chattels and had traveled here so that finally, after the fearful torments of seventeen weeks of brief encounters, she could move in with Kohoutek for good. She had settled her accounts, cleaned out her room, taken down from her bookcase all of Milan Kundera's books in Polish, Broch's *The Tempter*, Tatarkiewicz's *History of Philosophy*, and slim volumes of verse by Stanisław Barańczak and Ryszard Krynicki. With a perverse solicitude she had also packed the collected works of the greatest living Polish writer, whom she adored platonically, as a reader, and about whom Kohoutek was decidedly unplatonically jealous. Kohoutek was brutishly jealous, and he knew what he was about: The greatest living Polish writer belonged to the immortal generation of inveterate womanizers. In a word, Kohoutek's current woman had packed up her things and her books, handed her keys in to the landlady, gone to the bus station, bought a ticket, and come to Kohoutek's hometown. She had never been here before, but from what Kohoutek had told her she was intimately familiar with this community inhabited exclusively by adherents of the Lutheran faith.

Kohoutek is in the insufferably sentimental habit of telling his current women all about the Cieszyn region. They fix their gaze upon him and attempt, to no avail in his opinion, to suppress their excessive admiration, while he spins tales about the Partecznik, Dziechcinka, and Jurzyków; he tells of the house built by his great-grandfather, the master butcher Emilian Kohoutek, and of the lawn that was once the courtyard of the great slaughterhouse. It goes without saying that Kohoutek is fully aware that telling his current women about his native land is not merely an insufferable custom. Kohoutek is also aware that it is a ruinous one. In this case at least, thinks Kohoutek, watching his current woman cross the lawn, in the case of this unimaginable story I have good reason to think of my ruin. I was utterly wrong to have told her about the Cieszyn region; I shouldn't have said a word about myself; I shouldn't have given her my address, my name; I shouldn't have agreed to everything, promised her goodness knows what, shouldn't have spent time in her crazy company.

How futile, how rhetorically hollow, and, thank heaven, how short lived were Kohoutek's lamentations. He shouldn't have gotten on that A line express bus. He shouldn't have traveled a thousand times between one town and the other. He shouldn't have asked any questions, and he especially shouldn't have asked the first question: "Sorry to disturb you, miss, but what are you reading?" He shouldn't have worn down his central nervous system with inordinate doses of world. It was that simple. Kohoutek heard, or perhaps whispered, the first verses of his great song of woe; the recollection of the maw of that leviathan of an express bus, in which he had caught sight of her for the first time, passed through his mind, but nothing more. There was no time for even the most stylistically enchanting of threnodies. Kohoutek watched his current woman crossing the lawn, while at the same time his brain was working with deadly precision. Kohoutek was wondering if any of the inhabitants of the house had already spotted her.

Kohoutek's current woman might have been spotted by Kohoutek's mother. She might have been spotted by Kohoutek's father. She might have been spotted by the pastor's wife or by the pastor. She might have been spotted by Miss Wandzia or by Miss Wandzia's mother. She might have been spotted by Oma, Kohoutek's grandmother. The postmaster, Kohoutek's grandfather, as he took some fresh air, might also have come to the conclusion that someone closely associated with Kohoutek was on the lawn. Kohoutek's current woman might also have been seen by Kohoutek's child, and she might have been noticed by Kohoutek's wife. Anyone might have spotted her. But with a tiny bit of luck, or rather with a huge amount, it might be that no one had spotted her. The final preparations for Oma's birthday the following day were under way, and besides, since that morning, in fact since the previous evening, the attention of the household had been occupied by a two-liter jar of beef meatballs that Oma, Kohoutek's grandmother, had hidden somewhere. The matter was pressing, since the meatballs were to be consumed within eight days of purchase. Two days had already passed. Time was advancing inexorably toward certain definitive formulae: A two-liter jar of beef meatballs past its consume-by date meant an eternity exploding in sulfurous flames.

The pastor's wife had initiated the hunt for the missing meatballs when she asked at supper, "What about the meatballs?"

"What meatballs?" said Kohoutek's mother, answering a question with a question.

"The meatballs I bought yesterday; I'm asking because they're to be consumed within eight days of purchase, and two days have already passed."

"Oma"—Kohoutek's mother turned to Oma, Kohoutek's grandmother; his mother sat next to Oma and, because Oma was deaf, Kohoutek's mother would repeat what was said at the table a second time, loudly and distinctly. Kohoutek, though he could hardly be called a neutral observer of events, always had the impression that the members of the household were in the mysterious habit of passing utterances from one person to another—"Oma, where are the meatballs that the pastor's wife bought yesterday? I'm asking because they're to be consumed within eight days of purchase."

"They're in the refrigerator," replied Oma.

This had taken place yesterday, but Kohoutek remembers it as clearly as if it had been today. Kohoutek can see himself—yes, that's him, Kohoutek!—as he rises from the table, betakes himself to the pantry, opens the refrigerator, and looks inside. Many foodstuffs are arrayed upon the shelves lit up in that polar glare, but there are, incontrovertibly, no beef meatballs.

When it transpired that the meatballs were also not in other places accessible to mortals, everyone clearly understood what they had in any case already suspected. The meatballs must have shared the fate of the wieners, frankfurters, meatloafs, cutlets, smoked chickens, roasts, tripe, sausages, and many, many other dishes that Oma had diligently and, by and large, irretrievably hidden.

The previous day's search once again fills Kohoutek's head as it rests upon the windowpane. Though it happened the day before, now it seems to Kohoutek that it took place years ago. The search had taken up the whole of the previous evening and all of that afternoon. Yet as time passed, the search party, losing patience because of its lack of success, began to suffer from a loss of morale. Spectral emblems of apathy, ill will, and even rebellion began to manifest themselves above the heads of the weary sleuths.

If the truth be told, the pastor's wife took no part whatsoever in the search. Immediately after dinner (which comprised mushroom soup with pasta, minced veal cutlets, red cabbage salad, potatoes, and cherry compote), as soon as she had taken her last mouthful, after she had discreetly spat out the last cherrystone onto her saucer, the pastor's wife, annoyed and irritated by the upheavals caused by the ebb and flow of the hunt, changed and went over to the church hall to a meeting of her ladies' circle. The pastor announced that he would check to see if the jar had not been concealed behind the books in his study. With a somewhat exaggerated assiduity he closed the white-lacquered door firmly behind him and a dead silence immediately ensued, clearly indicating that once again inspiration had come to him and that he was, in an uncommon haste, hurriedly scribbling down the letters and the words of one of his fiery sermons. Oma, having secreted the meatballs, had herself disappeared no one knew where, or rather everyone knew, since it was probably the same place as always. Kohoutek's wife was studying foreign languages. Kohoutek's child was watching satellite television.

Kohoutek's grandfather was sleeping the avid sleep of a shortsighted man who only in his dreams can see things far away. Miss Wandzia was playing the violin, while Miss Wandzia's mother was spying on her through the keyhole because sometimes, instead of practicing, Miss Wandzia would play simple pieces from memory and at the same time would read a romantic novel propped open on the music stand. In a word, everything was as it always was.

Only Kohoutek's parents persevered with the search. But for the moment they were in the attic. From above could be heard the shifting of furniture, the creak of cupboards being opened and drawers being pulled out—the inimitable sounds that accompanied the uncovering of the most secret hiding places. Knowing how thorough his old folks were, Kohoutek was well aware that they were hardly likely to raise their heads and look out of the window. Either way, though, there was no more time to lose.

Kohoutek's current woman was walking across the lawn that had once been the courtyard of the great slaughterhouse. On her back she carried the backpack filled with her belongings, while behind her she dragged the suitcase full of books.

Kohoutek ran downstairs, silently crossed the hallway, pulled aside a piece of wainscoting, and, taking a secret shortcut he had last used thirty years before during illicit childhood games, passed onto the veranda. The smell of apples had the intensity of autumn thunder. Kohoutek opened the door of the veranda with its orange-tinted glass panels, and his feet stood upon the weary grass of November. Rounding the house, he began to run toward his current woman. Led by something other than himself, he was headed for the most apocalyptic assignation of his life.

Kohoutek always felt that Oma's birthday was a more important holiday than Christmas Eve supper, more important than the fast on Good Friday, than Easter breakfast, more important than New Year's Eve, than New Year's dinner, more important than Reformation Day.

On the afternoon of the day of her birthday in November, guests and members of the household would take their places at the table. Oma, wearing a navy-blue linen dress and a sheepskin jacket draped around her shoulders, would listen to the toasts with a serious expression and nary a flicker of a smile. Kohoutek's mother, Kohoutek's wife, and certain of the lady guests would be shuttling to and fro between the dining room and the kitchen, bringing in the successive courses. Miss Wandzia played the violin. They sang hymns from old hymnbooks. Dr. Oyermah gave one speech after another.

Oma's birthday was the introduction, development, and conclusion of yearlong plans. The very next day some of the dishes were returned untouched to the freezers. Kohoutek's mother once again ironed the spare tablecloths that had been prepared in case of accident and put them away in their time-honored places in the chest of drawers. The plan of the table drawn by Kohoutek's father on pasteboard, place cards to show who should sit where, and the sheet of foolscap with the script of Oma's birthday celebration—the religious part, the prayer, the numbers of the hymns, the toasts, the speeches, and the sequence of dishes—everything was conscientiously rolled up, folded, and stored in the dresser. It was stored for a short while, for a split second, for barely a single year. A year that went by with staggering rapidity, with all its heat waves, rains, and snowstorms upon the roof of the house.

Less than two weeks after Oma's birthday, Advent began, and preparations for Christmas proceeded with redoubled energy. Sometimes Kohoutek awoke at the darkest hour and even at four in the morning, in the blackest depths of the night, illuminated only by a few isolated lights from the spa spread out in the valley, he heard noises in the kitchen, from where he could smell cakes being baked. Christmas came and went in an unbelievable rush. The inhabitants of the house sat down to supper on Christmas Eve, went to bed, then at dawn Oma was put into a rocking chair, wrapped in blankets and rugs, and, by turning the ancient piece of furniture into a sort of Yuletide vehicle, a festive sleigh, our immortal if scarcely mobile Oma was given a ride to the morning service. There was Christmas dinner; before the New Year Kohoutek's mother baked doughnuts; New Year and Shrovetide lasted, it seemed, no longer than an hour or so, and you barely had time to catch your breath before it was Lent. The woods on the hillsides were still frozen, not one branch swayed, not one ice-covered blade of grass; yet it was Lent already, preparations for Easter were under way, right after Easter spring erupted. We old Lutherans, who are at the same time the real narrators of this story, cannot refrain from mentioning that in the Cieszyn region of Silesia spring has all the abruptness of a reformation—sudden heat waves sweep the length and breadth of the land like heretical fires. Kohoutek's mother would go out into the garden at dawn and come back at sundown to see to the meal. During the spring and summer there were over a dozen celebratory dinners: Kohoutek's father's birthday, Miss Wandzia's mother's birthday. Unexpected guests appeared, summertime tourists asked about rooms to let, and Dr. Sztwiertnia and his daughters came to stay for a few days. The earth underfoot was dry and loose as pine needles; the smell of mixed woods combined with the smell of suntan lotion; Barania Mountain burned and from the attic window the billowing smoke and orange-colored tongues of flame could be seen. The whole population stood on the summits of neighboring hills and watched the annual conflagration; only those couples who were lost in the tall Lutheran grass and plunged in ruinous Catholic lust were unable to pull apart from one another, and, motionless, literally at our feet, they awaited the end of the spectacle. August was already cooler, and the riverbed grew gradually darker; in September, on the most beautiful days there occurred frosts, while at dusk, when you took a deep breath you could detect in its smell the presence of the first snows lurking in the heavens. Oma's birthday was drawing near. The grass on the lawn, which had once been the courtyard of the great slaughterhouse, was turning yellow. Oma's birthday was growing closer with every day.

For as long as Kohoutek could remember, time had always constituted the anticipation of her birthday, which was coming up in a year. In six months. In a month. In a week. Tomorrow.

He ran around the house and saw his current woman passing in front of the huge dining room window. The light was on inside, the table was being laid for supper, and the drapes had not been closed. She walked straight ahead; she didn't yield to the most natural impulse in the world: She didn't turn her head toward the light that flooded over her, and she didn't glance into the illuminated interior.

Damn her, she knows I'm not there so she doesn't even look, thought Kohoutek to himself as he lurked behind the corner of the building. Dear God, I'm not taking Your name in vain, but how is it that that woman knows everything, always, everywhere? How does she know I'm not in the dining room?

When he finally caught up with her, he stepped forward and took hold of her hand. He didn't put his arms around her; he didn't say a word; he simply took her by the hand and, turning about, led her to safety.

They zigzagged across the checkerboard that the shapes of lighted windows marked out on the grass, keeping to the darkened squares. They walked quickly, almost running. Kohoutek's current woman was finding the going more and more difficult, and she was panting ever more hoarsely. Kohoutek did not take the backpack from her back, nor did he help her with the suitcase; in the desperation that had taken hold of him, he dragged her along behind him, tugging at her hand and over and again squeezing her fingers painfully. All this he did partly unconsciously, and yet partly on purpose, to punish her for the problems she had caused him by her outrageous arrival.

We old libertines, laughing as we observe this scene, yet filled with dread from a peculiar kind of sympathy, might add that Kohoutek's anger and desperation were undergirded by a rational cunning. Kohoutek was well aware that by hurrying to the aid of his current woman, he was, when it came down to it, increasing the risk and rendering the situation even more dramatic. Because now someone might not merely see his current woman on the lawn; they might equally well spot Kohoutek himself at her side. What was more, someone might also notice Kohoutek's absence from the house. At any moment a cry might go up: "Kohoutek, where are you?" Kohoutek's mother, for instance, seeing Kohoutek's cap in the hallway, might assume that recklessly as usual, as usual goodness knows why, Kohoutek had rushed out without his cap, and so she might, taking the cap with her, set off after Kohoutek; a thousand courses of events of this kind might take place. But there was one chance in a thousand that nothing would happen. And besides, let's be honest, despite the unpropitious circumstances Kohoutek was glad to see his current woman. He touched her and the same thing happened to him that always happened when he touched her. At such times Kohoutek was reduced to his own hands. Whenever he touched her, his whole existence was concentrated into his hands. Now especially, it can be said that as Kohoutek feverishly squeezed his current woman's hand, he was literally bearing his whole fate in the convulsive grip of his fingers.

He pulled her toward the old slaughterhouse. Kohoutek's current woman saw before her a thicket so dense that it looked to her like a dark mound; a tangle of fir, hazel, burdock, and sugar cane; an impassable barrier. But Kohoutek led her along a sort of path, and after a moment crumbling white walls began to appear through the vegetation. The door opened noiselessly and the lovers stepped into safe territory. Here, amid slaughterhouse machinery that was rusting like a seasonal monument, no pursuers were likely to catch them. Nevertheless, Kohoutek was still uneasy.

"We're going upstairs," he said and finally took the suitcase from the hands of his utterly exhausted current woman. "It's quite a weight," he growled reproachfully and led the way up the wooden steps.

When his current woman found herself in the attic, to begin with she could not comprehend what world she had come to. Kohoutek, though he had told her everything, never mentioned that his family had since time immemorial been in the habit of collecting basic forms of packing. First they amassed cardboard boxes; later came the plastic-bag period. There had also been a time of collecting paper sacks from sugar, flour, and rice, though rice was rarely used in Lutheran cooking.

Truly cubist expanses extended before the eyes of Kohoutek's current woman.

Who thought up the first cardboard container in the world? Who was the creator of the first box? For sure there must exist encyclopedists who know the dates and names of these inventors. For sure too on the second floor of that old slaughterhouse there could be found at least one box from the very first series. In any case there were containers from before the war with labels still legible: "Paweł Molin of Cieszyn: Groceries, Agricultural Supplies, and Building Materials," "Ryszard Płoszka's Bookstore and Stationer's, Jabłonków," "Scharbert's Department Store, Ustroń," "Fussek and Sons Glassware, China, and Haberdashery," "Amsterdam Brothers of Český Těšín, Woven Goods and Silk Stockings."

There were towering piles of German boxes with Gothic hiero-glyphs that Kohoutek's current woman was unable to decipher, bulky cubes marked "UNRRA," countless numbers of ordinary brown receptacles which had been used to pack Christmas presents or prison parcels, boxes that had once contained apples or fragile crockery, boxes that smelled of naphthalene, gray soap, or tobacco. Boxes that to this day retained the smell of the fifties, the scent of the first oranges and the first lemons. Boxes that came from un-specified periods and were covered in dust and spiders' webs.

Kohoutek's current woman's first reaction was to think that Kohoutek had led her to this container graveyard in order to tidy it up a little. For Kohoutek had in fact thrown himself upon the card-board pyramids with a singular zeal and had begun to toss them from one place to another. And Kohoutek's current woman was familiar with Kohoutek's fears and habits and knew that the princi-ple had been drilled into him that everything in life had to be earned by superhuman toil in inhuman conditions. She imagined to herself, then, that Kohoutek was attempting to deserve her arrival, to be worthy of her presence by the superhuman exertion of tidy-ing up the attic of the old slaughterhouse. When they had finished, when all the boxes had been properly stacked and sorted, they would go downstairs, cross the lawn, boldly enter the dining room, and Kohoutek would announce emphatically, "Mother, father, wife, and all you dear members of the household, this is my current woman, with whom I have tidied the attic. Goddammit, someone had to get around to it."

"Amazing," Oma, Kohoutek's grandmother, would reply, her voice filled with incredulous admiration. "The two of you tidied the attic all on your own? It must have cost you an inhuman effort!"

The other members of the household would in silent appro-bation make room for them at the table, and the unexpected arrival of Kohoutek's current woman would be legalized by means of the ethos of superhuman toil in inhuman conditions that had been lovingly cultivated in Kohoutek's family. But this was merely a daydream that passed through the head of Kohoutek's current woman, which was filled with the world of books. For he was grubbing around among the cardboard boxes not to tidy them up but in order to construct for her some kind of shelter or den.

Behold, my man is building a house in which we shall grow old together, thought Kohoutek's current woman, virtually without a hint of irony.

Kohoutek, in the meantime, was indeed laying down foundations and putting up walls. He worked with astonishing proficiency. In all probability, fear and panic had stirred in him the inspiration characteristic of great builders. In any case he gave the impression of being an experienced constructor of makeshift sleeping quarters. Once the bed was ready, he even fashioned over it something like a canopy, which in fact also had a practical purpose, since over the piles of boxes there was nothing but a crumbling ridge roof. For a moment Kohoutek thought about covering the provisional coping with plastic bags, but plastic bags were stored in the laundry room, and an expedition to fetch them entailed additional perils. Besides, even though the laundry room contained several thousand plastic bags at the very least, Kohoutek's mother was bound to notice if even a handful went missing. These days, now that the country had liberated itself from the Muscovite yoke and in almost every store purchases were wrapped in what were once priceless plastic sacks, Kohoutek's mother dropped by the laundry virtually every day to deposit a carefully folded new addition, and she was fully cognizant of the size of her collection. Here, on the other hand, in the loft of the old slaughterhouse, it was safe. In any case, no one had looked in here for ages. It had been ten years since the last cardboard boxes had been deposited. In those days European Lutherans used to send donations in them—coffee, tea, chocolate, shampoo, and washing powder—though, strange to relate, the smell had completely evaporated from those latest boxes. They didn't smell of martial law. They smelled of nothingness.

Kohoutek worked without a break and didn't say a word. His current woman sat on the suitcase, smoked a cigarette, and was silent too. Only when he had finished did he straighten up, wipe the sweat from his brow, and ask, "When did you arrive?"

"Now," Kohoutek's current woman replied.

Kohoutek was awake; he lay on his back and cogitated. What's to be done, dear Lord, what is to be done? Dear Lord, it's not that I'm taking Your name in vain, but for God's sake what's to be done?

Over the roof of the house the frenzy of the November night intensified; it was eleven o'clock in the evening, but at that time of year it was pitch black, the midpoint of a dark road with no turning back and no end in sight. The inhabitants of the house had long been sound asleep. Bright clouds are racing across the sky at a fearsome pace like canoes full of Indians; the eternally immobile hills seem to be entertaining all kinds of movement, while over there, in the attic of the old slaughterhouse, my current woman is sleeping, wrapped up in three woolen blankets.

What's to be done? What's to be done? What's going to happen tomorrow when someone notices that the three woolen blankets are not where they belong? And what's going to happen when

Mother notices that the bread has been cut crookedly and that a sizeable portion of hunter's sausage is missing? I'll say that I ate it. Even then there'll be a row because I ate it any old how, instead of setting the table properly first. The blankets are more of a problem. Any moment now someone will notice that three woolen blankets aren't where they belong, and then the fun will begin in earnest. The three woolen blankets are supposed to be on the wooden shelves in the stove room. At this time of year hardly anyone goes into the stove room; actually, hardly anyone ever goes into the stove room, but there's always the terrifying possibility that tomorrow someone might just pop in there. And if someone does, whoever it might be, Kohoutek's father, or his mother, or Oma, or Kohoutek's child, whoever it might be, there's no way they could fail to notice that three woolen plaid blankets are not in their place.

By the by, thinks Kohoutek, I wonder how it's possible that no one ever goes into the stove room and yet everyone knows that there are three Skoczów woolen blankets on the wooden shelves in there. A curious paradox. Kohoutek would like to pursue his inquiry, since he senses subconsciously that it may bring relief to his fraught nerves, but no such luck; there's no chance of relief, for yet another fear pierces his body and soul like a darkling blade: What will happen tomorrow morning when at the crack of dawn everyone continues the search for the two-liter jar of beef meatballs which they have thus far failed to find? They might start looking in the old slaughterhouse, and if they don't find it in the old slaughterhouse they'll climb up to the attic of the old slaughterhouse, and then they're absolutely sure to find something, only it won't be a two-liter jar of beef meatballs, but instead they'll find my current woman. True, I did build her a shelter which the most meticulous searcher would never find; but they, the members of my family—they're bound to find it.

Kohoutek turns on his side and assumes the fetal position; and, as always when he is in the fetal position, his thoughts turn to crime. Best of all, he whispers to himself, seized with a sudden rage, best of all would be to kill her. I ought to get up, go out, and kill her. When they find the body there'll be a row anyway, but not such a fearful one as if they'd found her alive. If they find her alive, there'll be such a fearful row that they're all likely to end up killing each other. Father'll try to kill me; Grandfather will defend me so Father will kill Grandfather; Oma will kill Father; Mother will kill Oma; the pastor will kill Mother; the pastor's wife will kill the pastor; then, taking advantage of the situation, since she's long hated her, Miss Wandzia's mother will kill the pastor's wife; Miss Wandzia will kill her mother because she doesn't want to play the violin; I of course will be killed by my own wife; and the long and the short of it will be that for weeks on end everybody will be offended with everybody else to the point that no one will be speaking to anyone.

The custom of death threats was an ancient one in the Kohoutek home. Kohoutek had heard immortal phrases about killing ever since he learned to listen. I'll kill you, Kohoutek's mother would say to Kohoutek's father. We should just kill her and have done with it, both of them would say when Oma had hidden yet another item of food. Practice or I'll kill you, Miss Wandzia's mother would say to Miss Wandzia. I'm going to kill him, Oma would say when once again Grandfather returned home three sheets to the wind.

Kohoutek had never come to terms with this domestic rhetoric of death, and each time he was seized by the most genuine fear that in the end someone would indeed get killed. Whenever he wandered through the endless corridors, hallways, and suites of rooms, whenever he looked into chambers into which no one ever looked, he was always afraid he would stumble across the body of one of the inhabitants of the house, wrapped in bloody plastic sheeting, or some inhumanly desecrated torso, hurriedly and carelessly covered with newspapers. As he walked into the garden, he was terrified that he would come upon a patch of freshly dug earth, and sticking out of it, as in a cheap horror movie, someone's dead hand.

Best of all, repeats Kohoutek, would be to kill her. Best of all would be to kill her and to hide the corpse properly; then there wouldn't be any row. Or at the very least I should have a serious heart-to-heart with her. I mean, during these few weeks we've never really had a decent talk. I told one lie after another and she went on and on about literature, Kohoutek admits to himself. What's to be done? Where can I put her? A hotel is out of the question, since everyone would know all about it at once. The entire town, inhabited as it is exclusively by adherents of the Lutheran faith, would know the whole story immediately. Maybe— the glimmer of a vague notion brightens Kohoutek's mind—maybe she could be passed off as a vacationer, and maybe they could be persuaded to rent out a room to her? After all, for years there's been talk of the money to be made from renting out rooms; every year hundreds of summer visitors ask if there are rooms to rent and are met with a sneering rebuff. Every time there's someone who won't agree to it, either Kohoutek's folks, or Oma, or Miss Wandzia's mother—though she rents a room herself, she's opposed to the other rooms being rented. But no one will agree, thinks Kohoutek, to my current woman. When they see her in that little curio of a hat, as one man they'll all be opposed to her renting a room even for an hour. What's to be done? thinks Kohoutek feverishly. How long will she be staying in the attic? I mean, she needs certain comforts; she has to wash, use the bathroom. How will I be able to handle all that? How could she do this to me?

All at once the floor creaked and Kohoutek sat bolt upright, because he thought he saw his current woman standing at the foot of his bed.

"Come here," he said with that particular sort of tenderness which human fury can sometimes turn into in the space of a few seconds. The specter standing at the foot of the bed vanished, but the tenderness remained.

Dear Lord, thought Kohoutek, dear Lord, it's not that I'm taking Your name in vain, but when all's said and done, my current woman is sleeping in the attic of a prewar slaughterhouse, separated from outer space by no more than a layer of crumbling roof tiles and a piece of cardboard. I mean, it's ridiculous.

At this point, in Paweł Kohoutek's soul and body deadly fear gave way to stupendous audacity. Since I was capable of concealing her; since I was able to take her bread, sausage, lemonade, and three blankets from the stove room; since I managed to accomplish all that, I'll accomplish even more: Unnoticed by anyone, I will go to her and I will make love to her, said Kohoutek almost aloud, and he rose from his bed. Incidentally, his thoughts continued, what is it that she sees in me? She's just like all the others; she's attracted by that damned veterinary medicine, he answered himself. In the silence and the darkness he set about getting dressed. He put on pants and a sweater, pulled his shoes on his bare feet, threw his trench coat around his shoulders, and moved off with extreme caution down the long hallway toward the front door. As he was passing the room in which his wife slept, he paused for a moment to assure himself he was safe. He placed an ear to her door and listened to her peaceful breathing. The poor thing's asleep, he thought, and he was suddenly overcome by another wave of emotion. This time it was an emotion connected strictly with the matter of marital fidelity. The poor thing, she's sleeping peacefully, and I'm up to all this. I mean, I've been with this woman for so many years, whispered Kohoutek to himself, so many years, and what I'm doing is so immoral. And upon a sudden impulse Kohoutek opened the door and, still dressed in his clothes, climbed onto her bed and began to shower her with passionate kisses. Kohoutek's wife, who was in a deep sleep, didn't immediately realize what was going on. But when she woke up fully, when she turned on the light and saw Kohoutek lying next to her in his trench coat and shoes, she spoke unto him the following words: "Have you lost your mind? Why are you all dressed? Has the one gray cell that until recently was rattling around in that brain of yours, has that solitary gray cell of yours finally disappeared too? Why won't you let me sleep? What disgusting things have you gone and thought up now?" Kohoutek's wife imagined that he had some kinky purpose in getting dressed; but Kohoutek wasn't really listening to her complaints.

"I love you, I love you, I love you," he kept repeating spasmodically as he continued showering her with kisses and feverishly pulling off her nightgown. And in the end Kohoutek's wife, who truth to tell didn't really have much of a thing for Kohoutek, gave in and allowed him to stay till morning. First, though, like a decent person he had to put his pajamas on.

We old libertines will make no bones about it: The next morning Kohoutek climbed up to the attic of the old slaughterhouse with an exceedingly dubious mien. Kohoutek could generally speaking be described as a man with a dubious mien, but this time his mien was especially dubious. After all, he carried with him the awareness that that night he had been unfaithful to his current woman. In addition, he realized full well that the latter, guided by her diabolic intuition, already knew everything. He was taking her breakfast—a thermos of hot coffee and a slice of bread and ham—yet even though preparing the coffee and the slice of bread and transporting it out of the house constituted a heroic feat, he was aware that this would little avail him. A stormy scene lay ahead. But so did an extraordinary surprise.

When he reached the top of the stairs, he beheld his current woman. Wearing a green dress which he had never seen before, she was sitting on one of the boxes; on her lap she had a jar of beef meatballs, which she was eating cold.

"No!" shouted Kohoutek. "Don't eat those!"

"Why not?" asked Kohoutek's current woman. "The consume-by date hasn't passed yet. I checked the label."

"Don't eat them! Don't eat them!" Kohoutek continued to exclaim. "Here, I've brought you some proper breakfast."

"So I'm not allowed to eat either," said Kohoutek's current woman. She set aside the jar and wiped her mouth carefully on a paper tissue.

"Where did you find that jar?" asked Kohoutek.

"In yonder box," the alleged culprit retorted in a sarcastic tone, pointing to a cardboard container that bore the inscription "Jan Buszek, Colonial Goods, Stelmacha St., Cieszyn."

"That's impossible."

"Please don't accuse me of lying; you know full well that I never lie," announced Kohoutek's current woman in a tone so frigid it portended the explosion of an entire iceberg.

"How many of them have you eaten?"

"Listen"—this time her voice took on a note of apparent con-ciliation—"I've only eaten one meatball; but I'll pay you for the whole jar." And with an ostentatious earnestness she set about digging in her purse, which, as if genuinely taken out in readiness for the settling of accounts, lay on a nearby cardboard box.

But Kohoutek was paying no attention whatsoever to the per-formance being played out before him. The fact that she's eaten one meatball is neither here nor there, he thought, analyzing the situa-tion. Naturally, it's a pity she opened the jar, but that can be hushed up; in the worst instance the blame will fall upon Oma. There's no need to make a tragedy out of the fact that she's opened the jar and eaten one meatball. And an indubitably positive aspect of the situation is that the meatballs have been found; in a moment I'll put them back where they belong, and the feverish search will come to an end. But it turns out that this place isn't safe! And that is a disastrous, even a tragic piece of information. How is it possible that

Oma, who walks with a stick and can barely drag herself around on her feet, managed to find her way up here? How is it possible that she was able to climb those stairs, as steep and narrow as a ladder? How is it possible that someone so infirm, someone who once a year has to be taken to church in a rocking chair, was capable of completing such a vertiginous ascent? Clearly anything was possible. Since it's possible that my current woman came to me out of the blue, and what's more came to stay with me for good, it's also possible that a frail old lady climbed the stairs with the agility of a monkey, concludes Kohoutek bitterly.

"It may not come to this, but you'll have to be prepared for it," he says to his current woman.

"And what precisely is it that I'm supposed to be prepared for?"

"Maybe tomorrow, maybe the day after tomorrow, maybe in a few days' time Oma will come here. There's lots of food in the house and she's bound to try and hide something again. I told you she does that from time to time."

"Very good," says Kohoutek's current woman, seemingly listening to her instructions closely, "when Oma appears here, what am I to do?"

"Hide."

"And what if she catches me by surprise?"

"Keep a cool head. Remember one thing. If she catches you by surprise, if she sees you here, it's entirely possible that she'll ask you the question."

"What question?"

"She'll ask if you're not by any chance Catholic, and you have to deny it and say that you're a Lutheran. That'll put her mind at rest."

"I told you just now that I never lie."

Kohoutek gazes at his current woman in silence and is suddenly stunned by a blindingly simple thought. Kohoutek realizes that his current woman is a lunatic. Kohoutek's flesh creeps. Surely no normal woman would ever come here under such circumstances, and yet she did come. So what is it about her, wherein lies the mental defect that leads her, permits her, to set out on an expedition so nightmarish both for everyone else and also, after all, for her herself?

"Fine, I'll handle it," says Kohoutek's current woman, this time in a tone that not only indicates the end of one topic but announces a transition to another. "You were with her again."

Kohoutek, who knows that it is pointless in such situations to put up any kind of resistance, however desperate, remains silent, and after a moment asks helplessly, as if in the hope that helplessness and confession of guilt are in fact his strong suit, "How did you know?"

"I can see it; I'm a woman." And all at once Kohoutek's current woman bursts into hysterical tears.

"You were with her, you were with her, on the very day when I came here, when I came here to stay with you for good!"

"I've told you umpteen times, there's nothing I want more, but at the same time things are not so simple." Kohoutek does indeed utter this assertion with terrifying facility.

"But you promised, you promised that we'd be together, that we'd live in this house together and we'd make our living by renting rooms to vacationers!"

"It's true, I did promise that," says Kohoutek reservedly, "but at the same time I indicated that for it to be possible, all the inhabitants of the house, or at the very least the great majority of them, would have to die. So those were not so much promises as vague dreams."

"You don't love me," whimpers Kohoutek's current woman.

"You know how much I love you," replies Kohoutek in a somewhat weary voice, since the conversation has taken a decidedly stereotypical turn. "I love you more than life itself, but I have to leave you now. You know that it's Oma's birthday today, and there's a huge amount of work to be done." Kohoutek stands, kisses his current woman on the top of her bent head, and, awkwardly, aware that his gesture has something of a gesture of confiscation, picks up the jar of beef meatballs.

"I'll come by this evening," he says.

As he is walking down the stairs, cautiously so as not to drop the jar, he hears a rustle above him. He looks up and sees the face of his current woman leaning toward him. Her features are distorted with such tremendous fury that Kohoutek is literally petrified with fear.

"Maybe I'll come by this evening too. I'll come by this evening to wish Oma many happy returns," Kohoutek's current woman spits out with a truly reptilian hiss.

It was true: Kohoutek was in the habit of setting out before any woman he came to know more closely a vision of their life together. This was the key to his successes. The women loved to hear tales of trips taken together, breakfasts eaten together, and, naturally, children raised together. We old libertines are well aware of the ancient banal truth, that the thing the vast majority of women most long for is stability, stability in the most general and the most strictly philosophical meaning of the word. Even women who seek adventure want stability above all else, since stability is the foundation and virtually the prime requirement for true adventure. Speaking in his dreamy voice of their life together, Kohoutek offered his women the illusion of stability. Even stable married women leading stable lives loved to listen to Kohoutek's stories, for it seemed to them that the life together that Kohoutek proposed would be even more stable. Furthermore, as Kohoutek set out before every woman he came to know more closely a vision of their life together, he was by no means lying. He was not playing some erotic game, nor was this some strategy for seduction. When it came to seduction, Kohoutek was a natural. He thoroughly believed what he was saying. At the time of the telling, he really did want to spend the rest of his life with the woman he was talking to. He really did imagine to himself all those details and episodes. This was the source of his credibility and his narrative proficiency. In his straightforwardness, Kohoutek was entirely unaware of the psychological contexts we have just mentioned. He would wake up in the morning at the side of a woman with whom the previous evening he had been planning a life together, and he would say to himself, Good grief, what a load of nonsense I came out with yesterday, and he would flee in absolute panic. In just such a way, willy-nilly, this erotic simpleton (there is no other way of labeling Kohoutek) had acquired a considerable series of sexual experiences. Yes, even we old hands in the bed department have to admit, not without a touch of envy, that Kohoutek had known a great number of women.

He had known wise women and he had known foolish women. He had known loose women and he had known virtuous women. He had known women who giggled like crazy in bed. He had known women who at crucial moments had almost died laughing. He had known prideful women who, irritated by the defenselessness they inevitably felt at such moments, became aggressive. He had known women who throughout the whole thing remained silent as the grave, and he had known women whose talkativeness rose in proportion to the intensity of their bodily excitations. He had known women who talked of nothing but sex, and others who would do anything yet treated any attempt to talk about sexual matters as an unbreakable taboo.

He had known a woman who liked to babble like an infant in bed. "Goo goo, boo boo," that particular ardent thirty-year-old would say to Kohoutek. "What id diddums doing? No, no, givey handy–pandy, givey, ooboodooboo," she would repeat over and over, and Kohoutek in his confusion would continue to do what he had been doing, though he had the absurd impression that for the first time in his life he was doing it inside a huge baby carriage that the brunette's efficiency apartment had turned into. Kohoutek had known a woman whose husband gave her rides to her dates. He had known a high school senior who, as an entrancing evening was coming to an end and a tired Kohoutek was ready to walk her to the taxicab stand, announced all of a sudden that she would have to wait for another couple of hours and drink some vodka, because if she went home too early and in a sober condition her parents would know immediately that something was amiss. Kohoutek had known women who went with him because they had been unhappily in love with someone else for years, as a consequence of which they would go with anyone.

He had known a second-rate singer, and his affair with her had been one of the longer affairs of his life. When Kohoutek woke up in the morning he didn't flee in panic, but stayed, and stayed for a good few weeks. The intensity and surprising longevity of Kohoutek's affair with the second-rate singer arose from his fascination with music. Kohoutek of course didn't know the first thing about music, and as far as a musical ear was concerned, he was spectacularly tone deaf. And yet music was a vital component of his erotic consciousness, or rather unconsciousness. It could be said that he saw music as a domain which lent women an exceptional charm. It could be said that he saw music as a peculiar and extraordinarily kinky item in a woman's wardrobe. It could be said quite simply: Kohoutek preferred female singers to male singers, female pianists to male pianists, female percussionists to male percussionists. There existed domains of life in which, in Kohoutek's view, the division of roles between men and women should run with truly stunning symmetry. Music was one such domain. Music, according to Kohoutek, should be composed exclusively by men, while it should be performed exclusively by women. There should simply not be any male singers operatic or popular, male choirs or even mixed choirs; all singing, to Kohoutek's mind, should issue exclusively from female larynxes. Music should be born in men's bodies, but should

31

be realized by the bodies of women. All musical instruments were also in essence created for women. Grand pianos, upright pianos, guitars, violins, trumpets, trombones, double basses, and all other music-making devices were basically intended for the female sex. When Kohoutek listened to music and at the same time saw the female pianist in a straight black dress rising over the keyboard, he was overcome with a paroxysmal sense of the equilibrium of life. The man (for it must have been a man) who for the first time handed a musical instrument to a woman was, in Kohoutek's opinion, one of the leading forefathers of the harmony of the world.

Who was the first female instrumentalist in the history of humanity, and what did she look like? What instrument did she play? Alas, Kohoutek generally imagines this scene to himself in a superficial, comic-book fashion: He sees a dainty blond dressed in animal skins being given a horn in jest by a fellow caveman. With unexpected desperation and skill, she puts the horn to her Paleolithic lips and blows.

Occasionally, however, a nobler version of this scene occurs to Kohoutek. It occurs to him that the first female instrumentalist was of the Jewish faith. The scene of the handing over of the biblical horn then becomes an apocryphal episode of the Exodus unrecorded in the Holy Scriptures.

The second-rate singer was not, of course, the first female instrumentalist of humanity. She was merely a descendant of hers, and by a crooked and extremely indistinct line at that. She was her great-great-great-great-granddaughter in the thousandth generation. And so Kohoutek's affair with her, though exceptional by his standards, could not last forever. It lasted a month. Then for a long time nothing happened in his life. That is, Kohoutek breathed, ate, drank, conducted endless discussions with Dr. Oyermah, worked, vaccinated animals, clipped dogs' overgrown nails, and treated coughing calves and horses with colic; he traveled to Kraków and back a thousand times; but as far as his dealings with women were concerned, nothing noteworthy occurred. A few insignificant conversations, chance encounters, casual meetings.

Right up until the moment when, on a sultry June evening, at the central train station in Kraków Kohoutek climbed onto an A line express bus which at that time of the day was almost empty. On board, a deafening female singer could be heard. The carefree driver had turned his radio up to full volume and the voice of Mireille Mathieu seemed to intensify the stifling air inside the bus. Kohoutek sat on the left-hand side. For a minute or two he gazed out the window at the walls and buildings of the town, slowly crumbling into dust and presently immersed in yellowish masses of heated air. Then he turned his head and saw a woman sitting in front of him. There was nothing special about her. He closed his eyes for a moment; the bus drove through the crossroads at Lubicz and Rakowicka, while Mireille Mathieu sang her head off. Kohoutek opened his eyes and stared absently at the divine outline of the skull of the woman sitting by chance before him. She raised a hand and straightened her hair, which was fastened in a loose bun. Kohoutek caught the scent of olive cream and with that scent a mighty enchantment descended upon him. Enchantment is all very well, he thought lucidly, but I should check out what she looks like. He stood up, crossed to the other side of the bus and sat down two rows in front of her, though—to repeat—on the opposite side of the bus. For a moment he watched out the window again; the bus drove around the Mogilskie Circle, and then Kohoutek, as if by chance, pretending to be curious about the new hotel that was being built, turned his head, looked . . . and indeed, it was Her. Admittedly she was reading a book, something Kohoutek wasn't fond of, but without a doubt it was her. She was the first female instrumentalist of humanity. She was the one who had blown the shofar as she crossed the wilderness with the people of Israel. She was the one to whom, in the Hart Inn, Kohoutek's great-grandfather, the master butcher Emilian Kohoutek, had presented in jest a trombone abandoned by a drunken musician. She was the one who, wearing a claret-red dress with a white collar, had climbed onto the stage with an uncertain step, where she was then joined by others emboldened by her example: Helena Morcinkówna (trumpet), Krysia Kotula

33

(accordion), Marysia Jasiczek (clarinet), and Nathalie Delong (drums), who was swathed entirely in Istebna lace. When Kohoutek saw her for the first time, he knew he had already seen her a thousand times. She had been the first Czech stripper he had secretly watched through the window of the Centrum café. She was the one who had sometimes sat alone in the Warszawianki, drinking one cherry vodka after another, as tears streamed down her face. She was the one who he had called so many times, then when she answered he would say nothing. She was the one who had taken confirmation classes with Kohoutek. She was the one who in the sixties used to go sunbathing near the Dębnicki bridge. She was the one who sometimes walked down Karmelicka Street in a banana-yellow dress. She was the one now riding the A line express bus.

Kohoutek, guided not so much by experience (his frequent liaisons with women had taught him nothing) as by his native instinct, changed places again. This time he sat right in front of her and without even attempting to pretend that his actions were accidental, he turned around and asked, "Sorry to disturb you, miss, but what are you reading?"

During the first prayer Kohoutek slipped out of the house and took his current woman some marinated herring. While the pastor was speaking, he sneaked over to her with a small plate of cold meat. As the first toast was being raised, Kohoutek was running across the lawn carrying a bottle of champagne. While the first hymn was being sung, he was climbing up to the attic of the old slaughter-house with a bowl of tartar sauce. When Dr. Oyermah began the first of a series of speeches, Kohoutek was tiptoeing across the veranda bearing a small portion of vegetable salad for his current woman. After he had taken her a substantial slice of walnut cake and, pleased with himself, was on his way back to the birthday party, he spotted a silhouette in front of the house. Kohoutek's mother was awaiting his return.

Pride and alcohol, thought Kohoutek. Pride and alcohol have been my downfall. And indeed Kohoutek, who was not normally one for hard liquor, had this time joined in every round of drinks and once or twice had even poured himself a sturdy measure in the kitchen and downed it in one. Alcohol had given him wings that evening; his current woman had graciously received the leftover delicacies he had brought her and had refrained from any malicious remarks. She lay wrapped in the three woolen blankets, drinking champagne straight from the bottle and reading a book.

Kohoutek had grown bolder and bolder, confident that in the general confusion no one had noticed anything; at the end, when the goulash would be served, he was even planning to take his current woman a whole plateful of hot goulash. Kohoutek, it might be said, was almost a happy man that day.

Yet now, when he spotted the figure of his mother standing in front of the house like the specter of final judgment, he realized that everything had come crashing down. If Kohoutek's mother was waiting for him in front of the house, it meant that she knew perfectly well, and may have known for some time, where Kohoutek was going and what he was doing.

"I know perfectly well where you're going and what you're doing, and I've known for some time," said Kohoutek's mother, as Kohoutek, stiffly moving his suddenly numbed legs, at last came up to her. (Kohoutek's mother's intuition was typical maternal intuition; she had nothing like the absolute, truly cosmic intuition of Kohoutek's current woman. Kohoutek's mother sensed his antics; the other woman knew everything.)

"You should be ashamed to be up to such tricks, and on Oma's birthday at that. You weren't listening to what the pastor was saying because you had to go sneaking off goodness knows where," Kohoutek's mother went on, "and it would have done you good to listen." Deep down, Kohoutek felt a sense of relief, the classic relief of the fugitive who is finally captured.

"I *was* listening," he replied in a feeble voice, "the whole time I was listening to what the pastor was saying."

"Right," said Kohoutek's mother. "In that case, remind me of what the pastor was talking about."

"The pastor was saying"—Kohoutek's answer was the answer of a fearful student standing before a strict teacher—"the pastor was saying that every object possesses its own smell and its own fragrance."

"Yes, and what else did he say?" his mother pressed him. "He also said that there are objects that absorb smell, such as a person's raiment, for example. A person's raiment absorbs that person's smell and retains it."

"What else!" His mother's voice sounded like the clatter of the rifles of a firing squad preparing for the final volley.

Kohoutek was silent for a moment, since, of course, he did not know what else; he had only been half listening to the pastor as it was, while he wrapped up a few slices of ham and sausage in a napkin, and then he had sneaked off goodness knows where. He did not know what else, but he took a chance.

"The pastor went on to say that we ought to absorb God's word and retain it just as raiment retains—"

"Silence!" roared his mother. "I'll have none of your blasphemies, you miserable blasphemer! The pastor went on to talk about the soul," she said, more quietly now, though with her characteristic venomous matter-of-factness. "The pastor said that more even than raiment, the soul absorbs every smell. You weren't listening because you had to run off to that damned attic. The pastor said that the soul is thirsty and drinks like a sponge and absorbs all the addictions of the body, and that the saying 'a healthy soul in a healthy body' is true. And what's your soul like?" she roared once again. "What's your body like? Why do you defile it?"

For a moment she pursed her lips, then began to speak again, this time in a whisper filled with dramatic confidentiality.

"Have you no pity for your wife? Have you no pity for your child? Have you no pity for your father? Have you no pity for me? Have you no pity for Oma? Why are you doing it? Why are you killing us all? Are you trying to bring our house to ruin?"

Kohoutek stood with lowered head; all his strength had left him, all his thoughts had vanished from his head, life within him had died, and he had grown indifferent to the world. It was all the same to him; it made no difference whatsoever what would happen to him and what would happen to his current woman. The depths of shame and humiliation into which he was about to be plunged were so bottomless that one could maintain toward them only the indifference of an object that has lost its last point of support and is plummeting into the abyss.

His mother was once more silent for a moment and then muttered in a startlingly calm voice, "You smell; you stink of that filth. Yes," she added with deliberation, "raiment absorbs the smell of the person."

Then there was a new pause in the conversation, this time a very long one. The final minute of silence before the final verdict.

"Fine," said Kohoutek's mother. "Today is Oma's birthday and we won't have any embarrassing scenes. The next time I'll kill you. Now give me all of the cigarettes."

"I don't have any—I just smoked the last one," replied Kohoutek in a flash.

"Paweł," said his mother (she was the only person to use his first name, and rarely at that; the rest of the world called him Kohoutek). "Paweł, don't start all over again." She had raised her voice once more. "Give me the cigarettes right now."

"I've hidden them."

"Bring them here this second; don't humiliate me and make me go and get them myself."

"Just a minute," said Kohoutek.

He turned and ran back where he had come from. Nimbly—for he was filled to the brim with the element of relief, which is lighter than air—he climbed the stairs. His current woman stared almost resentfully at his empty hands, having grown accustomed to the idea that on this evening Kohoutek was the provider of all worldly things.

"Give me your cigarettes," said Kohoutek, panting.

"I've told you a hundred times to stay out of my personal habits. You're tedious, you're really tedious, constantly forbidding me to smoke."

"It's not about that; smoke as much as you want, but give me your cigarettes."

"Kohoutek," said his current woman in a pained voice, "Kohoutek, have you gone bonkers? How can I smoke if I don't have any cigarettes?"

"Now, right now," moaned Kohoutek convulsively, "I need a pack of cigarettes."

"What for?"

"Dr. Oyermah's run out of tobacco and he's growing more and more violent."

"Kohoutek, go and buy some at the pub or borrow some from your neighbor. There's no way I'm giving you my cigarettes," said Kohoutek's current woman; she ostentatiously picked up the pack of Salem menthols in front of her and put them away in her handbag.

And then Kohoutek, who in his panic began to think he could hear his mother's footsteps approaching, for the first time in his life used force against a woman. After a short tussle, he grabbed the handbag from her, opened it, took out the pack of cigarettes (which fortunately was almost full), pulled out three and put them on a cardboard box, then added two more.

"I'll come and visit you much later this evening," he said and moved toward the door.

Kohoutek's current woman, who for a moment had been rendered speechless, all at once began screaming at the top of her voice, "You brute! Raising your hand to a woman! You brute! When you spend your days with animals you become one! You butcher, you cutthroat! You veterinarian! You explorer of cows' asses! Your hands always did stink of horseshit! Give me back my cigarettes, you pig farmer! I'm going to get changed and come there, to Oma's birthday party, and I'll ask your master Dr. Oyermah if he wouldn't be so kind as to give me one of my own cigarettes! I'll be there the second I get changed!"

But Kohoutek didn't really hear that cry, which filled the entire valley. And strange to relate, it seemed that his mother hadn't heard anything either. Without a word she took the pack of cigarettes from his hand, and together they went back into the house.

Dr. Oyermah was standing at the table with glass in hand, making endless speeches and not letting anyone else get a word in edgeways. When he spied Kohoutek and Kohoutek's mother entering the dining room, he immediately addressed himself to them. For Oyermah belonged to that category of talkers who perceived a topic deserving of a florid oration in anything his eye happened to light upon.

"Behold the dear grandson of the honorable lady of the day, and the worthy mother of the honorable grandson," said Oyermah, upon which, incredibly, he stopped speaking.

There followed a silence in which you could have heard a pin drop; the only sound was the indistinct, muffled shouting of Kohoutek's current woman which could be heard from outside. Yet no one paid it any heed; they all stared at the soundless Oyermah. Moments of narrative collapse may have happened to this man once every decade, or they may never have happened at all. Oyermah talked endlessly. He talked while he was standing, while he was sitting, while he ate, and while he drank. He talked as he worked and during his long hours of socializing. He talked as he walked down the street, for at every step he met someone he knew, and he knew everyone there. And yet now he had stopped speaking. His shock of gray hair flopped over his forehead and he opened his mouth once more, and everyone had the impression that the moment of silence had not been a collapse but merely a preparation, a taking of breath before a stupendous continuation. Oyermah did in fact raise his glass and begin his speech again in an even more resonant voice.

"Behold the honorable grandson of the worthy lady of the day, and the dear mother of the honorable grandson . . . ," he said, and once more stopped speaking.

This time the silence was absolute, since Kohoutek's current woman had also gone quiet. She's changing, thought Kohoutek in an oddly calm way. She's changing and, if I know her, she'll be here in a short while. But he too, Kohoutek, despite his divided attention and his jangling nerves, gazed at his master in dismay. Dr. Oyermah, a tall and broad-shouldered old man who well remembered the days of the Austrian Empire, stood speechless. The man who had traveled the whole world (with the exception of the Philippines) stood speechless. Franciszek Józef Oyermah, Doctor of Veterinary Medicine, who had treated countless generations of Protestant domestic animals; Kohoutek's teacher, he who had first shown Kohoutek how to take an animal's temperature, how to measure its pulse, how to file a horse's teeth, how to trim hooves, how to insert a probe into the throat of a bloated cow, how to employ a trocar, how to dress a mare's broken leg; a man in whom Kohoutek had unbounded confidence; old Oyermah, who drank every day and yet was never completely drunk; he, with whose illegitimate granddaughter, Ola Krzywoniówna, Kohoutek had experienced his first initiations; a man who over thirty years ago had presented Kohoutek with the mythical Book of his childhood; an indefatigable talker whose stories, repeated for the thousandth time, still held the listener in suspense; an expert on animal anatomies and human souls—had fallen silent. And if old Oyermah had fallen silent, that meant that he had taken a turn, that suddenly in the space of a few moments he had truly aged, that he had felt the burden of time, that—perhaps for the first time in his life—he had thought about the inevitability of death. All those sitting at the table more or less clearly realized that Oyermah's silence meant the end of an era, and possibly even the end of the world.

In the absolute quiet a distant voice was heard: Perhaps Kohoutek's current woman had begun her lamentations anew; perhaps

41

the river had suddenly begun to flow faster; perhaps the wind had stirred the branches of the lindens, beeches, and oak trees that grew behind the old slaughterhouse. Oyermah emptied his glass without a word and sat down.

After the birthday party, thought Kohoutek, I'll walk the old fellow home and I'll tell him all about it. Maybe he'll have some advice. If he doesn't, no one will.

The silence continued; still no one was saying anything. Someone filled their glass, someone gave a profound sigh. Someone's chair creaked; the wind was rolling ever more gustily across the roof.

"There's someone on the lawn," said Oma suddenly, and in the total silence her feeble old voice rang out loud and ominous.

"Someone's walking across the lawn," repeated Oma.

Kohoutek has the distinct impression that the profession of veterinarian was chosen for him long before he was born. As far back as he can remember (and it sometimes seems to Kohoutek that he can remember the gray-painted walls of the delivery room in which he was taken out of his mother's belly), people always said of him that when he grew up he would be a veterinarian.

"Yes, my little Kohoutek, when you grow up you'll be a student of the veterinary arts," Kohoutek's father would say to him. "It's a good and noble occupation, for you'll save animals and help people. You'll earn a good living. But remember"—Kohoutek's father raised a cautionary finger—"that superhuman exertions in inhuman conditions lie before you."

This was one of the most frequently uttered sayings passed from generation to generation in the Kohoutek family. Kohoutek's great-grandfather Emilian Kohoutek, the master butcher, may not have overused the saying, but in all certainty he was familiar with it. His son the postmaster, Kohoutek's grandfather, on the other hand, was not only familiar with the saying but pursued all its real consequences.

Kohoutek's grandfather had so often forced Kohoutek's father to perform superhuman exertions in inhuman conditions that with time he had instilled in him the conviction that any kind of exertions other than superhuman exertions in inhuman conditions were meaningless. As a result, any exertions that Kohoutek's father undertook contained an element of the monstrous bordering on a loss of humanity.

When old Kohoutek set about, for example, painting the house, everyone knew that he would not rest till he had finished. He would don a paper cap and, thus crowned, would climb his painter's ladder. There would begin a fearful drudgery. There would begin the great ritual of superhuman exertions in inhuman conditions. Like Moses on Mount Sinai, old Kohoutek would not come down from his ladder for several days. He painted without a break, his movements inhumanly rapid and efficient. He took his meals without coming down from the heights that he had ascended. He ate, moreover, most unwillingly, first for a long time resisting Kohoutek's mother's repeated entreaties and persuasions. In the end he would set aside the scepter of his brush, remove his crown, and agree to receive his handmaiden. She would climb gingerly up with small, respectful steps, bearing a tray before her. When she reached the immediate vicinity of the monarch clad in his armor of emulsion paint, she would raise her arms over her head. "Have something to eat, eat something, Duduś," she would whisper. Kohoutek's father would eat in great haste, indicating by the very carelessness with which he ate that he was against eating. In addition he ate in complete silence; he never uttered a word to Kohoutek's mother, let alone paying her any kind of culinary compliment or offering a word of thanks. Because his eating at the top of the painter's ladder was also a blow aimed at Kohoutek's mother, who, by preparing sustenance for him, by bringing it and persuading him to eat with her endless entreaties, had reduced to human proportions his super-human exertions in inhuman conditions, ergo had rendered those exertions partial, superficial, and even absurd. Little Kohoutek would watch terrified as his father's body gradually became overgrown with a limy rind. He longed with all his soul to be like his father, to labor superhumanly in inhuman conditions, but he felt in his bones that he was not equal to the task. He longed with all his heart to be a veterinarian, but he sensed that he would never become a veterinarian like Dr. Oyermah. He knew he would never be able to transform himself into a real, thoroughgoing veterinarian.

Oyermah paid frequent visits to the Kohouteks. It was a period when the stables and the cattle shed were filled with the smell of live animals, dark as the scent of moldering wood. Jonathan the horse, who suffered from every kind of bad habit, would be whinnying in the corner and smacking his lips. The deep breathing of Oma's two favorite cows, Mary and Elizabeth, could be heard. The male hog Douglas would grunt emphatically. Beltsville the turkey would be about to take flight, as Humphrey the cat crossed the tar-painted roof with the agility of a stuntman; while over the whole scene there arose the ceaseless hubbub of the common poultry, with its countless flocks of chickens, geese, and ducks.

"Chickens, geese, and small green ducks." Oyermah would croon the first bars of what seemed to Kohoutek to be the Great Veterinary Anthem, after which he would sit with Grandfather Kohoutek over a glass of rectified spirit mixed with hot caramel. The doctor addressed little Kohoutek as "my honorable successor."

"The time will soon come for you to begin your studies, my honorable successor," he would say. "I'm already gathering the necessary materials," he would repeat over and again, and, as it transpired, this was not idle talk.

One day in February, when the blinding flames of an almost forty-degree frost seemed to be turning the air to ash, Kohoutek spotted the characteristic figure in its immense sheepskin coat making its way through the snowdrifts in the yard (which was no longer the courtyard of the great slaughterhouse, but was not yet merely a lawn).

"So then, the time has finally come, Postmaster." Oyermah stood in the doorway, placed his immense case, with which he never parted, on the bench beneath the window, then crossed to the kitchen stove and began warming his cold hands over the range.

"That's right, the time has finally come, Postmaster," said Oyermah to Kohoutek's grandfather, who was sitting at the table. "Comrade Khrushchev has laid bare the despicable deeds of Comrade Joseph Vissarionovich, yet his joy will be short lived, for before long he too, Comrade Khrushchev, will be laid bare." Oyermah watched contentedly as Oma poured sugar into the ritual saucepan and set it on the stove.

"The regime, Postmaster, won't last the next forty years; not a year longer, and likely even less. We'll live to see a couple more Comrade First Secretaries, but no more, and not because we ourselves will pass away, Postmaster, but because there'll be no more of them." Kohoutek's grandfather was breaking the brown wax seal of the quarter-liter of spirit with professional precision. "There may be five more of them, maybe only four. We'll survive them all and we'll live to see those sweet times when the Chekist cap will be removed from Poland's head. We'll live to see it, Postmaster." Having finished warming his hands, Dr. Oyermah took a package wrapped in brown paper from his capacious case.

"We'll live to see times of such intoxicating freedom, Postmaster, that it'll all but drive us wild in our old age." Oyermah removed his sheepskin coat and tossed it nonchalantly onto the bench. "For we ought to remember that the Chekist cap conceals both the virtues and the shortcomings of our valiant nation. And when, in less than forty years, the Chekist cap will be taken from its head— and I assure you, Postmaster, that it will fly off us with the lightness of a chicken feather—when the cap is taken off, not only our considerable virtues, but also our colossal shortcomings will see the light of day. It's no use pretending: Difficult times await us, but we both know full well that there are no easy times. At most there are pleasant moments, like this gray hour, may it last forever," Oyermah concluded his speech, turned to Kohoutek, and handed him the package wrapped in brown paper.

"And this is for you, Kohoutek Junior, my honorable successor. It's time for you to begin your studies, if only with illustrations. Luckily the cow bringing its progeny into the world is free of political influences, and so the thing is still serviceable and has not been subject to revisionism. Although it's not strictly true"—Dr. Oyermah settled himself comfortably at the table—"it's not strictly true that a cow, that divine creation, is free of political influences. Because as everyone knows, if you give a Bolshevik a cow he'll just starve it to death," said Oyermah, and he suddenly grew sad, watching glumly as Oma poured the hot, oily drink from the small tin teapot into the glasses.

Kohoutek removed two huge, thick volumes from the brown paper. They smelled like the doctor—of alcohol and of the hair of domestic animals. Kohoutek was not familiar with the concept of "the mythical Book of childhood" (in fact, the term was not to be introduced to him till more than thirty years later, by his current woman), but that classic, ritual scene had undoubtedly just taken place a moment ago. Kohoutek had received from the hands of Dr. Oyermah the mythical Book of his childhood; he slowly turned its pages and at every moment met with incredible, breathtaking illustrations. Colorful plates depicted every existing kind of domestic animal, their cross-sections, their innards, their skeletons. In the detailed drawings, executed with a meticulous if somewhat heavy-handed realism, one could observe the anatomy of animals' limbs, heads, and torsos, and the systems of muscles, veins, and sinews. Kohoutek couldn't tear his eyes away from the truly terrifying images of sick animals; as if bewitched, he stared at a foal's hernia big as a head of cabbage, at cows' udders covered with the bluish skin of furunculosis, hooves foundering and festering or hypertrophic. Further on there were vivid, colorful pictures of affected limbs, poultry stricken by fowl cholera, animals sick with dyspnea and infested with roundworm, stomach worm, threadworm, tapeworm, and liver fluke. And more distinct details and close-ups: ulcerated tongues, crooked spines, edematous gullets, tetter the bloody red of a setting sun, abscesses yellow as sand on the beach, miry gangrenes, ulcers, and exudations. Dumbstruck, Kohoutek turned page after page and stared, horrified and fascinated at the same time, at animals sick with cholera, swine pox, and tetanus. The deformed heads of cows with lumpy jaw, the necks of horses suffering from mange, the larvae of heel flies big as tennis balls lodged in fur and skin. Naturally he did not know any of the terms and did not understand the captions underneath the illustrations; he turned the pages and encountered time and again apocalyptical images of incomprehensible animal suffering, pictures of animals motionless yet writhing in the mortal convulsions of poisoning by salt, arsenic, lead, phosphorus, copper, zinc, or nitrate.

At the beginning of the second volume, the anonymous artist had depicted a broad rural landscape: The sun was setting over green hills, smoke rose vertically from the chimneys of country cottages, while in the foreground a group of men were bustling about the monstrously bloated body of a dead horse. One of them was digging out the last spadefuls of earth from a huge, deep pit; another man was making an incision in the dead animal's skin with a knife as large and sharp as a sword; a man in a cap and tall army boots was pouring a white substance into the depths of other similar incisions; while another specialist, following after the others, was dousing the animal's remains liberally with a yellowish fluid. From the distance someone had run up bearing a burning torch. . . .

"So then, Kohoutek Junior," Dr. Oyermah asked from the table, "what impression has your first look into the depths of an animal's bowels made upon you? It's a tough sight, is it not?" Oyermah stood up and went over to Kohoutek.

"I see you're studying the ideal course of action to take with a dead animal. That is indeed what should be done: Make incisions, pour in lime, douse it with kerosene, burn it, and bury it deep. But what you see here is the ideal course of action. In reality—in that reality," Oyermah said with emphasis, "the poor little horse would long since have been chopped into pieces and gobbled up virtually raw. And soon afterward," added the doctor, turning the pages with a practiced hand, "soon afterward the noble visages of the collective farm workers gathered here would look thus." And Oyermah showed Kohoutek a hideous sequence of pictures of people suffering from various animal-borne diseases. "This one has *beshenstvo,* this one's caught *yashchur*"—Oyermah's finger passed from one repellent face to another—"this one has *rozhe,* that one *sap.* But I repeat once again that despite the fact these tomes contain a multitude of episodes remote from reality—from that reality—they will still be of service. See here, for example, Kohoutek Junior." Oyermah turned another few pages and before Kohoutek's eyes there flashed a number of black-and-white drawings showing the most ingenious veterinary instruments: lancets, probes, obstetric cauteries, chisels and forceps, saws, clamps, and curved needles. "See here, Kohoutek"—this time Oyermah found a page filled with innumerable images of horses' opened muzzles—"see, Kohoutek, my honorable successor. This is how you determine the age of a horse: from the state of its teeth. There, this little horse is a month-old foal, a suckling with its first two little teeth. But this one"—Oyermah's finger was once again moving across the breathtaking pictures—"this one has all its teeth and has spent at least half a year in this mortal life. While this one here is an old fellow with old teeth, occluded and flattened. An old fellow of more than twenty who's slowly preparing himself for his last gallop toward the great stables in the sky. Besides, there's little point in talking about the late years of animals, because domestic animals are in the fortunate position of almost never dying of old age. We veterinarians cut short their sufferings. We improve on the Lord God Himself, putting right the deficient invention that is the decrepitude of late old age. Yes, Kohoutek Junior, study these learned books, for soon there will come the time for a practical demonstration. If I remember rightly, before long Elizabeth is due to bring her offspring into the world, and you, my honorable successor, will stand at my side for the first time."

"Kohoutek," asked Dr. Oyermah thirty-odd years later as, after Oma's birthday party and the hunt for Kohoutek's current woman that had been organized in the garden, they were walking together down a road that led through the heart of a windy November night, "Kohoutek, who are you hiding in the garden; what astounding beauty has decided to pay you a visit? Who is it? When did she arrive, and how long has she come for? When I saw her face in the window, I was left speechless. I thought it might be the ghost of my late wife Józefina coming to me. Nothing of the sort! My dear late wife Józefina was such an uncommonly ugly woman that even if the next world possessed truly otherworldly, that is to say endless, capabilities in the domain of plastic surgery, she would never ever manage to look so beautiful and so young."

"So she came right up to the window after all, even though I imagined that I could hear her shouting or crying in the distance," said Kohoutek, lost in thought.

"That's right, you imagined it, while she came right up to the window and squashed her nose against the glass like a playful child. In that childlike gesture of a beautiful, grown young woman there was such extraordinary charm that I was dumbstruck. I, old Oyermah, was unable to raise a toast—"

"But how in the world did Oma spot her?" Kohoutek interrupted him.

"Haven't the foggiest," replied Oyermah, somewhat hurt since he had been gearing up for a lengthy tirade devoted to the subject of how he had been surprised at himself; besides which, he had a constitutional aversion to being interrupted. "Haven't a clue. I would guess that she didn't so much spot her as sense her. She sensed her and scented her with her old lady's luck. People whose senses are slowly on the wane, who are going deaf and blind, losing their smell and their hearing, sometimes have curious flashes of sensation. I'd say they're the last surges of a body that is inexorably dying. Surges that are farsighted and apparently supernatural; for a split second they hear or see something that no ordinary mortal can hear or see. Perhaps the honorable lady of the day all at once heard the crack of a twig beneath your beautiful friend's foot; perhaps she heard the rustle of her dress; perhaps she saw some shadow that was invisible to everyone else but her.

"You noticed, I hope," Oyermah continued after a moment, "that I did what I could to hold them back. Because when she looked through the window, she looked only at you, Kohoutek, and she did so with a gaze that was so fiery, so venomous, and at the same time so full of despair, that I did not have a shadow of a doubt: The person looking at you was connected to you by very special bonds. Who on earth is she, Kohoutek?" Appearances to the contrary, Oyermah was not yet expecting a reply.

"I knew right away, I knew that it wasn't an accident, that the lady outside the window hadn't wandered along by mistake, that she wasn't lost, that she wasn't someone led by idle curiosity to look through the windows of a lighted house to see what was going on. And so when there arose a great commotion around the table, I did everything I could to prevent a possible search. All the honorable guests and members of the household were extremely glad of the alleged presence of someone in the garden. They all froze—you noticed, Kohoutek, because you froze too—everyone froze in mortal consternation when I, Oyermah, fell silent. You thought that perhaps I was dying, weakening, that the end was approaching, that the fragile blade of decrepitude had suddenly run me through, whereas I had fallen silent out of rapture, out of youthful rapture, and also out of concern for you, Kohoutek, out of concern for the two of you."

It was true: When Oma had repeated once again that there was someone in the garden, everyone had leaped to the windows with an inordinate alacrity.

"Who! Where! On guard! It's a trick! It's a trick! Catch them! Hold them! To arms! Set the dogs on them!" they shouted, as if with the hurly-burly they had set in motion, the exclamations and the scraping of chairs, they were trying to fill the doctor's sudden and so meaningful silence. And it was to no avail that Oyermah unexpectedly rallied, that in a stentorian voice he called to them to resume the revels, that he tried to cool their fervor, that he attempted to raise new toasts; it was all to no avail.

The men flung overcoats across their shoulders; flashlights and candles were lit; weaponry was sought, canes, umbrellas, and skiing poles; Kohoutek's father dug a gas pistol from the depths of a cupboard, and old Oyermah, realizing that he would be unable to hold back such a mass movement, decided to take command and lead this ragtag army astray.

"Very well, officers"—Oyermah stood up and threw around his shoulders that same immense, eternal sheepskin coat, darkened and patched, it's true, yet the selfsame one—"very well, officers, we're heading into battle, but we have to follow the principles of military strategy. Postmaster, you stay on the terrace and cover the rear. Engineer Kohoutek"—this was how Oyermah always addressed Kohoutek's father, who was a surveyor by profession—"you'll take your Browning toward the old slaughterhouse, and we, the Reverend Pastor and I, will slowly circle the house. While you, Kohoutek, check down below." With a most peremptory gesture Oyermah pushed Kohoutek in the direction mentioned. "Ready? Ready!" Oyermah roared in a stupendous bass voice that could be heard throughout the entire Cieszyn region. "Kill them! Kill them!" shouted Kohoutek's father. "Don't kill them, take them alive!" replied Oyermah, and the manhunt gradually disappeared into the darkness.

Kohoutek's heart was pounding like a hammer as he followed the route indicated by the doctor; knowing his master well, he sensed a conscious strategy and a deliberate orchestration in his hammy playacting, and indeed he had barely taken a few steps when he saw her. Kohoutek's current woman was standing by the trunk of an old apple tree, visibly shaking with fear and cold.

"What are you doing, woman, what are you doing!" Kohoutek ran up to her. "I beg you, wait just a little bit longer, and everything will be sorted out. You know how much I love you." Kohoutek stooped down, put his arms around his current woman's divine thighs, and lifted her up. "I love you more than life itself; take hold of the branch; I love you, I love you; pull yourself up just a little further; everything will be sorted out tomorrow," whispered Kohoutek out of breath, "we'll be together forever and we'll never part; climb up a bit higher, there's a really comfortable fork right there; I love you," said Kohoutek, "that's good; have a little rest, and when it's all over go back to your place. I love you." He looked up and it really did seem to be a good hiding place, because nothing could be seen in the twisted limbs of the apple tree, which had never been pruned. Kohoutek's current woman did not say a single word. Kohoutek took another look and, when he couldn't see even a shadow, even the outline of a figure, he had the uncanny impression that the crown of the old apple tree had swallowed up his current woman, that she had disappeared once and for all, that she had climbed, first through the branches, then up steps in the sky, to heights from which there was no return. "Ho, hey ho, hello, hello," Oyermah's warning call was heard from above. "Hey ho, hello, hello, hello," responded Kohoutek. "Hello, hello, Helen-o." Oyermah's melodious voice was closer and closer. "Hello, hello, Helen-o," responded Kohoutek, no longer humming but actually singing. With the next step and the next breath the pastor's practiced baritone joined their duet. "Hello, hello, Helen-o, how goes the flock, hello, Helen-o, hello." Kohoutek's father emerged from the gloom with gas pistol in hand and though it was from him that Kohoutek had inherited his lack of musical ability, he too added his voice. "Hello, hello, Helen-o." The whole quartet sang the old shepherd's song and strode across the lawn that had once been the courtyard of the great slaughterhouse. On the terrace they were joined by the postmaster; then the women came out in front of the house and they all sang old songs of Cieszyn. They sang "Hey Freedom, Sweet Freedom," "My Father's House," "Through the Valley You Flow, O Olza"; they sang "O Kolin, Kolin"; they sang "She Drove the Oxen" and "Where the Czantoria Flows." And when they began to sing "Yesterday Was Sunday," Oyermah, who was completely at home there, without stopping his singing vanished into the house and a moment later reappeared on the terrace with a tray upon which stood glasses and a bottle of liquor, and as he sang—"Yesterday was Sunday, today's a sorry day, my head will ache on Monday, and stay all week that way"—he poured out the drinks, and without stopping his singing he began to drink to all those singing, and everyone downed glass after glass as they sang, and still singing a whole series of farewell songs they began to take their leave, hugging and kissing each other. "Goodbye, goodbye, my friend, until we meet again," they sang, and once again they said farewell and hugged and kissed each other, because in this house it was as if, with the end of Oma's birthday, a whole year was ending, and the next day a new one would begin, as if a great holiday was ending and another great holiday was on its way, as if the unfathomable elements of end and beginning were right at this moment joining together.

10

They walked through the heart of the November night. They walked along the broad highway that led through the heart of the Cieszyn region. They walked through the heart of the world. They passed the bridge, the train station, the post office where Kohoutek's grandfather had been postmaster; they passed the Spa Resort, the church, the parsonage where the pastor and his wife had once lived, the Piast Hotel, and the department store; then they turned toward the Partecznik, where Oyermah lived. The whole time Kohoutek continued to tell his story. He told about everything. He told about his adventures with women, his veterinary studies, about writing his doctoral thesis on *amorphus globosus*. Drunk and sentimental (time and again Dr. Oyermah removed from his jacket a metal hip flask filled with paschal slivovitz), Kohoutek reminisced about the days of his most distant childhood.

"Do you know, master," Kohoutek was saying, "that it was not until many years later, and truth be told rather recently, that I realized that the mythical Book of childhood you once bestowed upon me was the two-volume *Veterinarnyy Entsiklopedicheskii Slovar,* published in Moscow in 1950? That's right," repeated Kohoutek, "a Stalinist veterinary dictionary published by the Gosudarstvennoe Izdatelstvo Selskokhozyastvennoy Literatury was the great Book of my childhood. It's quite another matter that not long ago I noticed, or rather ascertained, a quite extraordinary thing: In that two-volume work published three years before the generalissimo's death, there was not a single photograph of him, not a single likeness! Yet wasn't Joseph Vissarionovich Stalin the greatest veterinarian of all time? Was he not the father of veterinary medicine? Master, how is this so, how can it be explained?" asked Kohoutek, but Oyermah did not answer.

Perhaps he was weary; perhaps he knew that the questions Kohoutek was asking were nothing but drunken rhetoric; perhaps he understood, or rather (let us, old admirers of Oyermah's wisdom, put the matter with greater certainty) he most surely understood that the time had come when Kohoutek wanted to know and had to know everything. Everything in the profoundly philosophical and most far-reaching sense of the word.

"Maybe the thaw came earlier in veterinary medicine," mumbled Kohoutek, "who knows, who knows. But either way, master, you must have plodded thoroughly and purposefully through that work. To this day you still use Russian terms. I've never heard you say 'hernia'; you always use the term *gryzha.* Instead of 'burn' you say *ozhog;* 'swelling' in your language is *vzdutie;* 'rabies' is *beshenstvo;* you never just say 'founder,' but always a masterfully accented *vospalenie kopyt;* for 'murrain' you say *chuma;* instead of 'foot-and-mouth disease' it's *jashchur;* 'hog cholera' is *rozha;* 'glanders' is *sap;* 'tetanus' is *stolbnyak;* 'blackleg' is *shumyashchyy karbunkul,* 'anthrax' *sibirskaya yazova,* 'mange' *chesotka,* 'staggers' *vertyachka.* ...And what's *amorphus globosus* in Russian?" asked Kohoutek, who seemed to have fallen into some kind of lexical trance. "What's *amorphus globo-*

sus in Russian?" he repeated. "No one knows," he replied to himself with drunken resignation. "Even in that encyclopedia, as massive as any Stalinist edifice, such information is missing. . . .

"You remember, master, my first practical initiation into the mysteries of our art; of course you remember, because you remember everything. I was woken up late in the evening, though it seemed to me that it was the middle of the night like now; I was dressed unusually warmly though it was August, an old raincoat was put around my shoulders even though it wasn't raining, and I thought that this must be some kind of ritual clothing, that just as a bride has to have a veil and a white gown, so a veterinarian attending the birth of an animal has to be dressed warmly and wear a raincoat. Yet you had no raincoat or sweater on, you were naked; that is, over your bare body you wore a rubber apron thick as a car tire which reached down to the ground but left your torso and arms uncovered; you were lying on the ground and looked like a mythological Titan. Your right arm was plunged up to the armpit in Elizabeth's insides, and it looked as if you yourself had just emerged from the cow's belly and it was only in the last phase of your return to the world that your arm had become stuck in some obscure recess of the bovine anatomy. In the brownish light of an uncovered lightbulb, in the misty aura of animal excrement and human sweat you were thrashing about, calling on the Lord God; you were uttering such gruesome curses that I hardly understood a thing and I began to think that you would never free your imprisoned arm, that you would remain forever fused with Elizabeth, that in a veritably mythical turn of events you would be transformed into half man, half animal. I felt sorry for you, because I thought that for the rest of your own life you'd be in thrall to Elizabeth's life, that you'd have to go grazing with her, spend the night in the cowshed, and receive guests there, greeting them with your left hand and apologizing for doing so. I felt terribly sorry for you, and I was just about to burst into bitter tears when you, master, freed your arm with uncanny facility, and along with your arm there emerged from Elizabeth's innards a wet, oval-shaped form all covered with hair. Then I thought that out of this bizarre creature, as if out of an egg, at any moment there would leap a nimble, sprightly young bullock with silver horns and golden hooves. I was surprised that your fury continued unabated; when I saw a knife long and sharp as a sword in your hand, I thought you were going to make an incision in the skin to permit the newborn creature to enter the world, but to my horror you took a swingeing blow and with an imprecation on your lips you sliced in two the thing that was lying at your feet, and I saw an unimaginable tangle of veins, sinews, and undersized bones. My blind gaze passed over the insides of the shapeless anatomy. Liver, heart, and kidneys formed an indivisible unity; there wasn't even a lot of blood. The whole was simply steaming a little, as if letting out its first and last breath.

"Oma took me by the hand and led me into the house. It was a hot August night; I looked up because I thought I'd see Sputnik flying overhead, but there was only a white wilderness of stars and planets. The round shape covered in wet fur was now growing within me, rising, riding up into my throat."

Kohoutek fell silent. They came to a stop for a moment. Oyermah handed him the hip flask. Kohoutek took a long draught, and, as often happens after another shot of liquor, he began to speak in a lighter, calmer voice.

"That's right, master, it could be said that my career as a student of the veterinary arts began under an unlucky star, under the shapeless planet of *amorphus globosus.* Later, of course, I grew accustomed to monstrosities; we both often saw everted brains, piglets missing a lower jaw, Siamese births fused together, one-eyed foals, skulls distended with hydrocephalus. We saw many an example, we saw many an example of what you, master, would call an *urodstvo ploda.* But that image of the *amorphus globosus* cut in two never left me. All the more so because in the mythical Book of my childhood, on page four hundred seventy-seven of volume two, there is a picture of it, accurate and vivid like all the illustrations in that Book. 'Globular amorph. *Amorphus globosus (wneshnyy vid), Akusherskii Muzey Kazanskogo Veterinaryyskogo Instituta,*'" Kohoutek recited from memory.

They stood in front of the sports center, where for many years there had been gatherings of generations of ever-younger and -fitter women discus throwers, sprinters, and volleyball players who had achieved ever more impressive results. Kohoutek stared greedily through the darkened windows, on the other side of which the latest team of female pentathletes or hurdlers was asleep, and suddenly, with drunken ease he changed the subject. From the topic of his professional initiation he switched to that of his corporeal sufferings.

"Women," he said, "my current women. I won't deny it. In a restaurant I was always more interested in the waitress than in the dish she brought. I stepped into a pub not for a glass of beer but to be able to stare at the woman behind the bar for a quarter of an hour. I'd go to church; I'd pray and sing hymns, but the whole time out of the corner of my eye I'd be continually squinting at the profile of the well-groomed Lutheran lady sitting next to me. I'd get on the train and keep looking from one compartment to the next till my efforts were rewarded. I'd go whenever I was summoned to a sick animal, yet it wasn't the animal I was thinking about as I took its temperature, but about the lady of the house or her thoroughly grown-up daughter.

"Yet does all this mean it's only in their presence"—Kohoutek gestured toward the building filled with sleeping sportswomen—"it's only in their presence that I am transformed from an *amorphus globosus* into a rational creature? Is it only then that my expressionless face takes on some expression, that my lungs fill with air? Is it only then that blood begins to circulate within me, my jabbering speech becomes fluent, my existence takes form? I don't know, master, I don't know. I don't even know if I'm really Paweł Kohoutek, veterinarian. There's only one thing that I know beyond the shadow of a doubt: I'm possessed by the perpetually insatiable demons of touch."

They moved slowly forward again. Oyermah continued to be silent, continued to allow Kohoutek to speak.

"Pretty much throughout my whole life, I'd say"—Kohoutek seemed to be gradually sobering up, or he may have been sinking into an ever-greater drunken despair—"pretty much throughout my whole life, I'd say, I've done everything I can to be as much in their vicinity as possible. I always ran valiantly and untiringly along, following the trail of their perfume; I was rendered sightless by their effective or ineffective hairstyles. I reached out my hands to touch, plunging my fingers into the great rivers of consolation that run across their skin. I'd watch a woman going down Szewska Street; she'd be wearing a salmon-colored skirt and a white blouse; she'd be walking along with a quick, determined step, and the movement of her legs, her breasts, her hair would make me start to choke; I'd be suffocating on the world; I'd be suffocating and so I existed; I'd begin to exist; I'd choke on my first mouthfuls of air, while she was walking on toward the Market Square, and I'd turn around; I'd follow her trail, tracking her perfume; I'd stare at her calves; I'd stare at her hair tied in a bun with a nonchalance ordinary mortals cannot achieve; she would raise her arm, her hand, smelling of Evasion perfume, would straighten the barrette in her hair—it may have been that she, the woman in the salmon-colored skirt, or perhaps her hand smelling of Evasion perfume, understood the reasons, knew why I was choking on her, on the world, why the yellowish air of that city so enraptures me. It may be that she knew which of the possible answers was correct. I didn't."

Kohoutek fell silent and a moment later said with an unexpected desperation in his voice, "Fine, I accept that I'm just a common philanderer, the most ordinary kind of adulterer. A low-grade Casanova, a second-rate Don Juan. Fine, so be it: That's all that interests me; it's all I think about; I accept it, though that's an over-simplified and ugly way of stating the truth, because after all it's not the case that I bring myself down to my own genitalia, that I reduce my current women to their erogenous zones; quite the opposite, it's precisely at such times that infinity opens up before me; at such times God is close, for in the Gospel according to Matthew the Lord Jesus saith, 'Where two come together, I am between them. . . .'"

At this moment Oyermah coughed and it was most clearly a cough indicating dissent, but Kohoutek appeared not to hear it.

"That's right," he went on, "at such times infinity is within reach of my senses, that's what I think, but so be it: I accept the trivial opinion. I'm a lecher. I'm the most ordinary sex maniac in the world. But tell me please, why am I like this? What makes me be? Which demon am I led by? Why do I have the insufferably sentimental habit of telling my current women all about the Cieszyn region? Why do I promise every new woman I meet a life together? Why is it that, even though I know I'm lying, I imagine that I'm telling the truth, and I imagine that alleged truth so intensely that I end up thinking that it truly is the truth?" Oyermah continued to be silent, and Kohoutek continued to talk.

"I've tried, of course I've tried to understand the reasons; I've tried to establish some kind of rules for the game played between me and my proclivities. But I gave up, because the same thing happened that always happens—every theory fit me.

"It may be that I valiantly and untiringly followed their trail because in every woman I'm searching for my mother. It may be that I'm a closet homosexual. It may be that my conquests are intended to compensate for my lack of fulfillment. It may be that they're supposed to compensate for the fact that I'm more of a theoretical veterinarian than a real veterinarian. It may be that it all arises from the fact that I don't drive a car; I don't own a boat; I don't use a computer and the only complex device I'm familiar with is a woman. It may be that I'm suffering from—I hope I'm not misusing the word—a neurosis, and I've a neurotic need for love. It may be that in the depths of my guts or perhaps the depths of my soul I hate women and that's why I devour them so greedily. She"—Kohoutek gestured in the direction of his house—"my current woman, whose face you saw at the window, reckons the real reason is that I don't write, that I'm not a writer. My current woman maintains that all the women I've been with are substitutes for the novels I've never written. But that's nonsense"—Kohoutek shook his head disapprovingly—"that's nonsense. I get bored even reading books, let alone writing them. Reading books bores me and tires me, because, master, my eyes can only move very slowly."

They turned to the left and entered the valley of the Partecznik. The stream ran alongside the road; in the absolute darkness there could be heard the murmur of its waters, swollen after the recent rains. It was not far now to the old wooden house where Oyermah lived, and Kohoutek, as if coming to, began hurriedly telling what he had wanted above all to tell in the first place.

He began to tell about his current woman: about their first meeting on the A line express bus, about how he had gotten out at her stop and had walked her all the way to the doorway of the tower block where she lived, how they had stood in that doorway for maybe an hour, maybe two, until in the end a taxicab came by, as if sent specially for them by the angel or, as it was to turn out later, the demon, of their mutual attraction. Kohoutek is absolutely convinced that it was an infernal vehicle, originating in hell, sent from hell itself. Its color and make were hellish: a yellow Volga of the kind ridden by party dignitaries in the seventies. Cars of that kind had long since vanished. . . . But at that time neither she nor he realized that there was anything unsettling in their situation. They got into the yellow Volga, returned to the city, had dinner at Poller's, then once again went back on the A line express bus, and to cap it all it was the same bus they had taken before, with the same driver, which, in Kohoutek's view, could also have been considered further evidence of the existence of a conspiracy of evil forces.

Standing on the steps to Dr. Oyermah's house, Kohoutek told of subsequent meetings; he told of their quarrels that began unexpectedly soon; he complained that between him and his current woman there stood a huge mountain of books, of which she had read every one, while he had read only two or three, and really only because she had told him to. He said that when he touched her, he became utterly lost in his own hands, but he immediately explained that this was no ordinary sensual fascination. He told of the extraordinary love skirmishes in which she would seem to be melting utterly in his arms; then a few minutes later, when all seemed to be on the right, even the rightest of roads, it was as if she woke up, regained consciousness, and then began to offer such furious resistance that Kohoutek was thoroughly disoriented and lost all his strength, his enthusiasm, and his abilities.

"The longer these ever more ferocious struggles go on, the angrier I get," Kohoutek was saying, "and I start to behave like an awkward sixteen-year-old, or even worse."

In the end Kohoutek would pretty much give up and when he began his last attempt, devoid of faith or hope, she would unexpectedly lose consciousness once more, sinking into his arms, and yielding to the boundless pleasure that swept over her; Kohoutek recovered his strength, his enthusiasm, and his abilities and once again everything was on the right, even the rightest of roads, when suddenly, a moment later she would wake up again and begin to resist like a lioness, and so on endlessly for seventeen weeks, complained Kohoutek. But he added right away that he liked being with her, that he wanted to be with her; he liked being with her so much that he thought he loved her, though that was rather out of the question, because he, Kohoutek, loved only his wife, and he didn't believe that one could love two women at the same time—that was a typically bookish invention.

"It turns out that she has nothing to do with music," said Kohoutek. "I don't think I've ever even heard her humming anything, but that's of no consequence; she's still the leader of the Great Pageant of Female Instrumentalists, or at any rate she marches at the head of all the female percussionists, all the damsels playing their timbrels. As the psalmist says: 'The singers went before, the players on instruments followed after; among them were the damsels playing with timbrels.'"

"Or as it says in Ecclesiastes: You have gat you men singers and women singers, Kohoutek, and other pleasures of the sons of men. . . ."

But Kohoutek seemed not to hear the irony vibrating in Oyermah's voice. He continued to tell of the dozens of excuses he had thought up to be able to go and visit her; he confessed that as always he had promised her everything, a life together; he told her fantastic things that he believed when he told her them.

"But I never believed that she was capable of such a desperate measure," said Kohoutek. "When I saw her crossing the lawn with her backpack and suitcase, I thought I was seeing a ghost." And he went on to tell where he had concealed her and how he had brought her three woolen blankets and taken her food and drink; he told about the conversation with his mother, which had so fearfully complicated his trips to the attic of the old slaughterhouse; he told everything in detail, right up to the events of an hour before, when he had helped her hide in the branches of the old apple tree.

"What's to be done, master, what's to be done?" he asked helplessly. "Why did she come here? I mean, no normal woman," he repeated with cheerless obstinacy, "no normal woman would come here, and she did, so maybe she's not normal?"

Oyermah's shoulders were slowly beginning to shake in an attack of the giggles, which a short while later was to grow into an unbridled stentorian guffaw.

"What's to be done; I'm too weak to chase her away, and even if I decided to do so, she's still too strong to allow herself to be chased away! How long is she going to stay? A hotel, renting a room, I've considered everything and nothing is possible!"

Oyermah's laughter could already be heard all around.

"O lecherous Kohoutek," said Oyermah through his laughter; he was standing above Kohoutek, leaning on the railing of the wooden veranda that ran around the house. The lamp he had turned on a moment before illuminated his whole figure brightly, and it looked as though Oyermah the actor was standing on a stage and making a speech to an audience hidden in the shadows.

"O lecherous Kohoutek, what misfortunes have befallen you! Look at him, all of you," Oyermah roared at the top of his voice; he raised his hand, took the lamp with its tin shade hanging on a cord, and directed its light right at a startled and pallid Kohoutek.

"Raise your heads, rouse yourselves!" Even in this situation Oyermah was incapable of passing up the opportunity for one more tirade that evening. This time it was the Great Admonition to Lechers.

"Raise your heads, rouse yourselves, wake up," called Oyermah, and lights did in fact appear in the windows of two of the neighboring houses. "Wake up and imagine to yourselves that the nightmares tormenting you have become a reality. Imagine to yourselves that your current women are knocking at your door, introducing themselves to your wives, greeting your children. Imagine to yourselves that your fleeting adventures, your momentary fascinations and holiday romances are moving in with you! Raise your affrighted heads, both you experienced womanizers and you beginners. Raise your heads too, you who will never become womanizers, though you know that is what you were created for. I speak to you in a mighty voice"—Oyermah addressed himself directly to the growing number of lights being turned on, and to the shadows appearing next to them—"I speak to you in a mighty voice, for I hear a whisper telling me to speak in a mighty voice! Raise your heads, you sordid clerks seducing your coworkers, you lascivious bosses making your female staff members the victims of your desires, you editors preying on your proofreaders, you directors forcing yourselves on your secretaries, raise your heads, and you too, you lewd doctors, conquerors since time immemorial of subordinate medical personnel," fulminated Oyermah. "Raise your heads and listen. Do you hear that hammering?" Oyermah began furiously pounding on the door of his own house. "Those are your lovers, those are your current women, whom you have promised unheard-of things, and who have finally decided to talk matters out with you. They've come to your homes and they're knocking at your doors! When you hear that apocalyptic banging, when you stand petrified in mortal immobility, and when a moment later you realize with relief that that deliberately inflicted hailstorm is growing silent and dissipating with the rest of your nightmare-ridden dreams, perhaps you will look with due care at one of your own to whom this very turn of events actually happened." Oyermah once again directed the beam of light upon Kohoutek. "Take a good look at him! He has heard the hailstorm and has seen his current woman walking across the lawn."

Oyermah fell silent and for a short while seemed to be waiting for the round of applause that should follow; then he spoke to Kohoutek in the most normal of voices.

"Forgive me, Kohoutek. You know my weakness for sermonizing, and you know that it's stronger than me." The doctor stepped down and put his hand on Kohoutek's shoulder. "Forgive me," he repeated. "You asked me a whole mass of questions," he continued in a calm and matter-of-fact tone, "and in fact I could try and respond to them all right away; but I won't do so today. First of all, we're both tired. Second, the hour is late. Third, I'm convinced that your ill-starred lover is still sitting in the tree and waiting for you. She's waiting for you to come back and help her to return to earth."

Kohoutek gave a shudder, because he realized that the doctor was indisputably right. His current woman certainly would not dare to jump down from the branches of the old apple tree, especially in total darkness. After all, she was always exceedingly cautious even when going up stairs, moving with a charming awkwardness and always (Kohoutek recalled the countless climbs up the stairs of her apartment building with its eternally broken elevator), always clutching on to the handrail like grim death. He was about to turn immediately and run off, but he felt Oyermah's hand resting upon his shoulder and holding him back for the moment.

"There's just one thing I have to make clear to you right away, since as you know I'm fond of precision. Though reading books tires you and bores you, Kohoutek, when you do it, at least do it attentively, especially when you're reading the book entitled the Holy Scriptures. In the Gospel according to Matthew, the Lord Jesus does not say, 'Where two come together, I am between them'; He says, 'For where two or three are gathered together in my name, there I am in the midst of them,' and that means something rather different. Unless of course," he said slowly and deliberately, staring Kohoutek right in the eye, "unless of course, Kohoutek, your relations with your women are conducted in the name of the Lord?"

"Well, in any case they're not aimed against Him," retorted Kohoutek, suddenly irritated.

"You're breaking His Commandments." Oyermah uttered this statement in a whisper.

"But I believe in Him," cried Kohoutek desperately. "I'm breaking His Commandments, and it may be that He is angry at me, but so much the better, because in anger He exists more strongly and I believe in Him more. The Scriptures also say: 'They that are in the flesh cannot please God.' Yet I, Kohoutek, am in my flesh and women please my flesh, because of which I don't please God. But that doesn't mean that God doesn't please me. I'd rather He was angry or even cantankerous than benevolent. It seems to me that I believe in Him truly, and true faith is not an easy thing. Only fools and simpletons think that true faith is as simple as anything."

"Kohoutek," said Oyermah with paternal forbearance, "at the birth of Our Lord there were both wise men and shepherds. And the faith of the wise men and the faith of the shepherds was equally pleasing to the Lord."

"Well, I'm neither a wise man nor a shepherd," responded Kohoutek fractiously.

"It's an eloquent testimony"—Oyermah was almost amused—"it's an eloquent testimony to your modesty that in contrast to the vast majority of the world's population, you don't consider yourself wise. Though from what you say it sounds as if there lurk within you the makings of a speculative thinker, and that if you didn't waste your time chasing skirts and concentrated instead on truly important matters, who knows, Kohoutek, if you wouldn't become an ordinary rogue? In any case, I can assure you that to a much greater extent than we think, we are all of us shepherds.

"Kohoutek," said Oyermah a moment later, in a tone that indicated the definitive end of the conversation, "call and see me in the next day or so. Come by and we'll consult, debate, and ponder together on what's to be done. And now, shepherd"—he slapped Kohoutek on the back in a farewell gesture—"now, shepherd, run off back to your shepherdess and take her down from the tree before she freezes to death on you."

12

Even though her feet were almost touching the tops of the highest blades of grass, she was afraid, she was afraid of the last step into the unfathomable abyss. Kohoutek took her in his arms. She put her arms around his neck and embraced him with all her strength, clinging to him spasmodically as if he really had saved her life. And when it came down to it he too had the impression that he had rescued her from the brink of a precipice, saved her from drowning, carried her out of a burning house. And, since he was Kohoutek, what began as an impression turned into an ever-firmer conviction of the truth of his imaginings as they approached the old slaughter-house. Another few steps and he genuinely believed that if he had come even a minute later it would have been too late.

"What a relief, oh, what a relief that I made it after all," he whispered to himself in his heart.

His current woman was as frozen as a heavenly body. He felt the damp of her green dress (which he had never seen before) and the coldness of her cheek, and it seemed to him that her frail arms were chilled to the marrow. And suddenly Kohoutek understood for the first time that she was there, that she really existed. He comprehended her existence, because he had been made aware of her mortality.

"She'll die one day," he thought, "it's not possible, but certain; in fifty, or sixty, or eighty years she'll die and she'll have to be buried." Kohoutek was brought up short, for the few decades that his current woman still had to live seemed to him a terrifyingly short time, as short as one year, which was as short as the twinkling of an eye between one of Oma's birthdays and the next, and in his consternation Kohoutek determined to do everything he could to prolong the life of his current woman.

"You have to take a hot bath," he whispered in her ear. He suddenly turned about; he swayed, but kept his balance and set off toward the house. He stood her carefully by the window of the immense bathroom, which was in the basement.

"Wait a moment," he said and looked at his watch. It was three in the morning. In the house everyone should be asleep, everyone except his mother, who was bound to be still washing the dishes. I'll go into the kitchen and say that when I was walking Oyermah back home I mustn't have been properly dressed, because I got chilled to the bone, Kohoutek thought. I'll say I'm shivering and that my throat's sore, and so I'm going to have a hot bath and take some aspirin before I go to bed. When I say this to her she'll undoubtedly be overcome by the feeling of satisfaction that overcomes all prophets when their prophecies come true. (Kohoutek's mother was indeed forever predicting various illnesses for him, in consequence of which every one of his illnesses represented one of her predictions coming true.) However—Kohoutek continued to plot—she won't let it show that she has been overcome by the kind of satisfaction known only to accurate fortune-tellers; she'll just say,

"Who won't obey his dad and mom will end up feeling rather dumb; how many times have I told you not to dress too lightly," and then she'll fall silent, stop talking to me, and pay no more attention to me. As a punishment she'll leave me alone with my illness and at least an hour'll go by before she knocks on the bathroom door.

And Kohoutek's word became flesh. He went into the kitchen, where his mother was washing the dishes, and said, "I mustn't have been properly dressed as I was walking Oyermah back home, because I got chilled to the bone; I'm shivering and my throat's sore. I'll have a hot bath and take some aspirin before I go to bed."

Kohoutek's mother said nothing for a short while (during which time she was filled with the transparent element of satisfaction), after which she snapped, "I'm doing the dishes!"

And she fell silent, and paid no more attention to him. She left Kohoutek to his fate, punishing him for his foolishness. While he, a little out of countenance because the dialogue had not entirely played out according to his plans, went first to his room. He opened the wardrobe and took out warm long johns, a fustian undershirt, dark blue corduroy pants, a black-and-white-checkered flannel shirt, warm socks, and a huge lambswool sweater as big as Oyermah's sheepskin coat. He also providentially took his own pajamas and dressing gown, and thus burdened made his way to the bathroom. He locked the door, ran hot water into the tub, opened the window, and helped his current woman to climb inside. He smiled at her, took a white bath towel from the shelf, and was opening his mouth to repeat to her in a firm yet caring voice, "You have to take a hot bath," when an energetic knocking was heard at the door.

"Yes," said Kohoutek, petrified.

"It's me," came his mother's voice. "Open the door, there's something I want to tell you."

"I'm in the tub already."

"Open up, there's something I want to tell you," repeated his mother in a tone that brooked no resistance.

Kohoutek took all his clothes off in a trice, jumped into the bathtub, splashed his face and arms, jumped out again, wrapped a towel around his hips, and, nodding to his current woman to show her the safest place in such a situation, cracked the door open.

"I wanted to tell you that we're—" His mother broke off, seeing that something was amiss with Kohoutek. He was hopping from one foot to another, shaking, and making abrupt movements as if he were fighting with an unseen opponent. Kohoutek was indeed fighting. His current woman, who was standing behind him hidden by the door, was tugging with all her might at the towel that he had wrapped around himself.

"You're shaking all over," said his mother. "You're running a fever and you'll be lucky if you get away with a bout of pneumonia. Who won't obey his dad and mom will end up feeling rather dumb. How many times have I told you not to dress too lightly? We're out of aspirin," she added after a moment, "there's only Polopirin. It's on the kitchen table. Good night."

"Good night," said Kohoutek and closed the door.

His current woman was standing in the corner, covering her mouth with the towel in which up till a moment ago he had been wrapped. She was laughing, laughing ever more impetuously, ever more convulsively; her laughter seemed a distant echo of Oyermah's recent laughter. She was laughing and gagging herself with the white bath towel; in the end she took a couple of steps and, virtually tottering with laughter, sat on the toilet seat. After a moment she raised her head, and in her slightly asymmetrical features there was no trace of merriment; she stared for a short while at Kohoutek in his nakedness, then said in a flat and very quiet voice, "You have no shame."

Then when Kohoutek bent down to pick up his clothing from the floor, she nodded toward the almost full bathtub.

"Since you've already been in, go ahead, you take your bath first. I'll wait."

And Kohoutek, who had suddenly been seized with entirely real shivers and shakes, plunged into the hot water without a second thought. He washed himself while she folded her arms and waited motionless. Then she stood up, looked in the bathroom cabinet, checked whether the hair dryer was working, pointed it at Kohoutek, and said, "Bang bang." She went up to the bathtub, sat on the rim, touched his soapy arms with her forefinger, and stroked his wet hair.

"My poor skinny thing," she whispered. Kohoutek felt a lump in his throat; he realized that he was incapable of speaking, and that any second now he would burst out crying like the Great Romantic. He dipped his face in the water so his tears would not be seen and rinsed the soap from his hair and his arms.

"Don't get your dress wet," he said, also in a whisper, and made a gesture that was intended to indicate that he wanted to move her delicately aside. Then she reached out her hand again as if she meant to caress him gently once more, but no, this time she seized him painfully by the hair, leaned over, and hissed right into his ear, "You bastard, you've not said a word till now about my dress; you haven't even noticed that it's new, you bastard."

"I did notice," he said, grimacing in pain as she continued to pull his hair with all her strength. "I did notice; it looks really good on you."

"Yeah, right," she muttered contemptuously. "I don't believe a word you say. Get out already." She let go of him and, now seeming to pay no attention to him whatsoever, she began in an uncommonly meticulous fashion to examine the things that he had brought, which were lying on the washing machine. One by one she touched, smelled, held up to the light, and wordlessly replaced long johns, undershirt, shirt, pants, socks, and sweater. In the meantime Kohoutek dried himself, put on his pajamas and dressing gown, and let the water out of the bath.

"All right," said Kohoutek's current woman. She leaned over and with the same implacable meticulousness with which a moment ago she had been examining the garments brought by Kohoutek, she set about scrubbing the bathtub. Kohoutek sat on the toilet seat and watched her inhumanly rapid and efficient movements and realized that his current woman reminded him a little of

his father, old Kohoutek. Everything she did, she did with an inhuman fervor, and she would not rest until she had finished. That's
right, thought Kohoutek, she won't rest till this whole story finishes
in the way she wants. She turned her back on him and took off her
dress. For a moment she stood without moving and then said,
"Don't look."

Kohoutek turned his face to the wall and sat still. Behind him
he heard the splashing of water and for a minute he imagined that
he was on the deck of a great sailing ship. The passengers and crew
had all fallen into a deep sleep, while he alone, Kohoutek, was
leaning over the side of the ship and staring into the darkness.

13

"It's high time we gave some serious thought to taking in lodgers," said Kohoutek over supper in a voice trembling with anxiety. "Winter's on its way; there'll be crowds of skiers, quite a few of whom will be looking for somewhere to stay, and there's no lack of empty rooms here."

"That's right." Kohoutek unexpectedly found the postmaster, Kohoutek's grandfather, taking his side. "Young folk will be coming into town, and young folk should be supported, because they are our future."

"If we were to let a room to someone nice"—Oma, Kohoutek's grandmother, was sipping at a cup of tea—"then at least there'd be someone to talk to around here."

"Well, you can just kill me"—Kohoutek's mother was as white as a sheet—"kill me and bury me, and if not then I'll kill all of you. Don't you know what it means to let a stranger into the house?"

"What does it mean?" asked Kohoutek, taken aback by his own courage.

"What does it mean? It means the end. Sit up straight, sit up straight; if someone sees you slouching like that then you've had it. Letting a stranger into the house means annihilation for every one of us."

"He'll keep turning on the light"—Miss Wandzia's mother spat out the litany of crimes hatefully, word by word—"he'll make food, he'll wash in the bathroom, he'll use the toilet. . . ."

"Isn't it better"—Oma broke off a piece of dry bread and dipped it in her tea—"isn't it better that he should turn on the light and use the toilet, rather than relieving himself in a corner in the dark?"

"Sure it's better!" Kohoutek's mother spoke so quietly it seemed that at any moment now she'd pass out with rage. "Sure it's better! Sure, just what I need is for someone to make a mess in the bathroom or the toilet, all day long, woman, clean up after some filthy stranger, and at night don't fall asleep for a second, because you never know if he won't come and murder every last one of us."

"There's no denying it"—Kohoutek's father strove to lend his voice an exceptionally commonsensical tone—"there's no denying it, you never can tell who you let in under your own roof. Myself, for instance, if I saw some bum lazing around the house till midday, I'd kill him on the spot."

"There you are, if you want Duduś to spend the rest of his life"—Kohoutek's mother threw everything into the balance—"if you want Duduś to spend the rest of his life behind bars, be my guest, rent out rooms."

"That's right," Kohoutek's father said forcefully. "I'd do time, but I'd kill that bum on the spot."

"You're all heartless," Kohoutek's mother began to weep, "if you're trying to throw me out of the house, but go ahead, rent out my room; I'll move out right away; I'll pack my things right away; but I beg you, I beg you, just let me finish my last supper. Don't be so pleased, Duduś"—she turned to Kohoutek's father—"don't be so pleased about killing him, it would be him who'd kill you, but for them it means nothing to rent out a room to a murderer."

"Tough," said Kohoutek's father. "It's him or me."

"Or maybe"—Kohoutek's wife retained a studied calm and consequently tried not to look in the direction of her desperate husband—"we could let a room to some stylish, well-groomed lady?"

"Or maybe," Kohoutek's mother aped her, "we should just hang a red light over the door and be done with it? How do you like that—in one room the Rostov Ripper, in another the whore of Babylon."

"The Rostov Ripper was caught by the police." Kohoutek was truly in despair; he was kicking himself for setting in motion this discussion, which was clearly leading to a disastrous conclusion.

"So what?" Kohoutek's mother's surprise was virtually authentic.

"So," the postmaster, Kohoutek's grandfather, helped him out with a reply, "it's rather unlikely that some guy locked up in a Russian slammer would come here on a skiing trip and rent a room at the Kohoutek house."

"Don't be angry, Father, but you're just like a little child. How do you know that the person who knocks at our door to ask for a room isn't a serial killer? What do you think, that he'll introduce himself to you: 'Good morning, Postmaster. I'm a degenerate. Can I have a room?' Or maybe you think that he'll show you his I.D. card, and in the place marked 'occupation' it'll say 'woman killer'? No, he'll come in the night and murder you." The compassion with which Kohoutek's mother spoke was boundless.

"Why would he kill me?" the postmaster, Kohoutek's grandfather, defended himself. "I'm not a woman."

"I know," Kohoutek's mother said slowly and almost calmly, "I know that you're all thinking about me, and that you can't wait for me to die."

"Please don't get upset." The pastor's wife had been silent up to this point, sitting motionless with her head bowed and her gaze fixed on her empty plate; now, however, she sat up straight and sparks danced in her handsome eyes. "Please don't get upset; no one wants you dead or wishes you any harm."

"I know, I know," twittered Kohoutek's mother, "you and your husband don't wish me anything bad; but how can a stranger be let into the house without a second thought?"

"Now you've made your mother cry!" roared Kohoutek's father all of a sudden. "Your mother's weeping because of you; do I really have to kill you to stop you from doing that again? Do it one more time," he added more quietly, "and it'll be your head I come after."

"Don't you raise your hand to him, Duduś." Out of the blue Kohoutek's mother came to his defense. "You know how long it took him to get over the scarlet fever."

"It's not a question of letting a stranger into the house without a second thought, but of maybe, with a lot of thought, taking in someone we know." The pastor's wife had waited patiently for the end of the hate session.

"Who are you thinking of?" asked Kohoutek's mother, wiping her tears.

"I think, for instance, we could quite safely accommodate some retired pastor in this house."

"Another retired pastor?" Kohoutek's mother, who tried never to evince surprise at anything (people who were surprised by something were showing their weakness—they were brazenly demonstrating to the world that they didn't know everything), this time gave the impression of someone taken aback.

"That's right, another retired pastor," confirmed the pastor's wife.

A full minute of silence ensued—a minute of silence, thought Kohoutek, honoring the memory of the idea, buried in its infancy, of having his current woman come and live in this house—after which Kohoutek's mother burst out with ecstatic enthusiasm, "I can accommodate not one, but two, three, four, a whole group of retired pastors. Lord, how splendid it would be: an entire house full of re-tired pastors. Truly a time of joy would be upon us!" and Kohoutek's mother, almost literally exploding with uncontrollable rapture, sud-denly stood up and started singing:

A time of bliss and happiness
Has come to earth from heaven
Our Savior, our redeeming power
To sinful man is given
He's born to us this day
To drive our woes away
He'll guide us ever, so we'll never
Go astray.

She stopped singing, sat down, and said somewhat embarrass-edly, "It's too early yet for Christmas carols, but I'm so content, I'm just so content."

"Excuse me, ma'am, but specifically which retired pastors did you have in mind?" Kohoutek's father asked the pastor's wife.

The pastor's wife looked at the pastor, who was plunged in thought. It seemed that he was absent in spirit, and that, whispering soundlessly to himself, he was polishing the phrases of his next sermon; but no, the pastor cast a warm and shrewd gaze over all the inhabitants of the house and said, "For instance, the Reverend Po-traffke is retiring from the new year, and would doubtless be delighted—"

"Potraffke?" interrupted Kohoutek's father. "Reverend Potraffke has had three heart attacks, and, begging your pardon, Pastor, is likely to give up the ghost any day now. . . ."

"That's right, that's right," Kohoutek's mother confirmed. "The doctors aren't giving the Reverend Potraffke more than a month. There'll be a funeral!" she exclaimed enthusiastically a moment later. "There'll be a funeral!"

"The Reverend Konderla is coming up for retirement soon," came the next candidate.

Kohoutek's mother waved her hand impatiently, while Kohoutek's father's voice contained a note of persuasion laced with annoyance.

"My wife and I saw the Reverend Konderla's X rays; he has a tumor the size of a soccer ball."

"Malignant too," added Kohoutek's mother with a bewitching smile. "And it's spread."

The pastor's hands were trembling slightly; nevertheless, he maintained a good-natured smile.

"How about the Reverend Śniegoń?"

"Śniegoń, by all means," agreed Kohoutek's mother joyfully, "we can let a room to Reverend Śniegoń; out of politeness we just ought to wait for Mrs. Śniegoń to die. She has an advanced case of diabetes and makes no attempt to keep to her diet. It won't be long. Oh, I'm delighted that we've finally settled it! We'll let a room to the Reverend Śniegoń. Just as soon as he's a widower."

"While I," said Kohoutek's father, "am in Olympian condition."

"That's right, that's right," confirmed Kohoutek's mother. "Duduś is a real Hercules."

"Congratulations, congratulations." The pastor gave a curiously sad smile. "We're almost the same age, but my case is much worse—I'm in a bad way; I can barely get around. Rheumatism, gout, headaches, insomnia, kidney problems."

"Whereas I," said Kohoutek's father, "am in good health."

"Or we could rent a room to some lady teacher from the high school," said Oma, returning to a topic which had seemed to be definitively resolved and finished.

"I don't know, I don't know," wavered Kohoutek's mother. "I don't know whether we'd find the space."

"We'd have to find space for a teacher from the high school," said the postmaster in an unexpectedly vehement tone. "Teacher, doctor, and vicar: Those are sacred professions and space should always be found for them."

"A doctor? A physician?" Kohoutek's mother's euphoria and state of bliss vanished as if at the wave of a magic wand. "Out of the question! Are you trying to turn my house into a hospital, Father? An emergency ward? A delivery room? Out of the question! Now, a lady teacher from the high school we could think about, if by chance a room were to become available." Here Kohoutek's mother looked involuntarily at Miss Wandzia and at Miss Wandzia's mother, but she turned her head away immediately, and her startled gaze fell upon Kohoutek as he sat hunched over the table.

"Paweł, don't slouch. A person should sit up straight; a person should be in the image and likeness of the Lord."

"Don't give him such unattainable models," said Kohoutek's father with the satisfied voice of a gold medalist. "It's enough for him to be in my image and likeness." He took Kohoutek's mother's hand and placed it on his own heart.

"Can you feel that pump working away?"

"I can, Duduś!" replied Kohoutek's mother admiringly.

Kohoutek's father stretched, imitating the movements of the lion—king of the beasts—as it prepares to pounce.

"That's right," he repeated. "I'm in Olympian condition. Someone who walks well," he continued, "should be able to cover five kilometers in an hour. The table we're sitting at is five meters long and one and a half meters wide; in other words, its circumference is thirteen meters. But I will be moving in a considerably wider radius, so I can assume that a single lap of the table is fifteen meters. Therefore, in order to go five kilometers around the table, it's necessary—within the space of one hour, of course—to complete 333.33 laps. But I," said Kohoutek's father, "can complete 333.33 laps in thirty minutes." And he stood up at once and, with the unparalleled adroitness of a professional walker, swinging his body with great energy and waving his elbows wildly, he began to circle the table.

Kohoutek felt that the darkness into which he had been staring not so long before was now within him, filling him up to the brim. He felt that it had taken the place of his bones, his muscles, and his guts. He felt that instead of blood, darkness was circulating inside him. The inhabitants of the house sat in silence. From behind their backs there came the rapid, springy footsteps of Duduś the Olympian and his ever-hoarser breathing.

14

"I'm the cause of all your unhappiness, and you're the prime reason for all my unhappiness," Kohoutek's good-looking wife said to him. "It's our own fault."

Kohoutek's wife was wearing a black overcoat with red trimmings; her dark hair fell about her shoulders, while in her hand she carried a rose on a very long stem. They were going to the cemetery to place the flower on the grave of Kohoutek's great-grandfather Emilian Kohoutek, the master butcher. Their gloomy child trailed behind them.

"I don't want to make things difficult for you—in fact, I'd like to help you—but I have to confess that I'm sick of your perpetual betrayals, your perpetual chasing around after other women, your perpetual difficulties with yourself."

Kohoutek's wife was speaking composedly and matter-offactly. It was the sort of composed matter-of-factness characteristic of women who are both extraordinarily beautiful and are aware of their beauty.

"Most marriages have their problems," she continued, "but the heart of the matter is that when it comes down to it I'm not at all sure if this is a real marriage. Our problem is more basic. Forgive me, but when I'm at your side I sometimes feel like an old maid or—though I wish you everlasting life, Kohoutek—like a widow."

How is it possible that everyone except me knows everything about me? thought Kohoutek. Why is it that I keep asking questions and find answers to hardly any of them, while the rest of humanity, with my relatives and current women in the fore, knows the answers to every asked and unasked question? How is this possible?

"It's all because we met too soon"—Kohoutek's wife seemed to be answering his next question—"we met too soon, we fell in love too soon, and we got married too soon. And also because we didn't manage to part soon enough."

They were slowly climbing the high hill upon which the Protestant cemetery lay. It was an icy Sunday morning. Any day now, any moment now snow would begin to fall and frosts would come, and then the road to the cemetery would become a steep, slick, rocky path covered in snowdrifts and impassable. For this reason, for generations winter had not been a time of death in those parts. Old Protestants tried not to die in the winter. They waited for the eruption of spring, for the time when the softened earth would begin to swallow their light oak caskets like a warm lake. Those who were preparing for their final journey and had not managed to set off in the autumn had before them the last winter of their lives, and like any other winter they spent it fruitfully. As much as their strength allowed they helped about the house, practicing their German, for who knew if in the vineyard of the Lord they would not meet Dr. Martin Luther, and if they did it would only be right to say at the very least: "*Guten Tag, Herr Doktor Luther; ich bin ein Lutheraner aus Weichsel in Polen.*" And in the evenings, gazing at the frozen world through the window, they would tell terrible stories of winter funerals which had nevertheless occasionally befallen certain unmindful locals. There were stories of mourners sinking up to their waists in snow, of caskets slipping from their numb fingers, of despairing widows who, stumbling on the icy rim of the grave, fell into it as if driven not by accident but by desperation. As these stories were told there would be gargantuan laughter—people would simply die from laughing—and Kohoutek, who had heard a good many tales of this kind, smiled involuntarily.

"There's nothing funny in what I'm saying," said his wife.

"I smiled because I was remembering all those great funny funeral stories."

Kohoutek's wife looked at him serenely.

"Kohoutek, you're a big boy now; you should know what's appropriate and what isn't."

They reached the wooden gate and entered the cemetery. A steep gravel path passed among the graves; the gravestones rose in tiers up the hill as far as the horizontal line of the old quarry. Down below, the river flowed around the flank of the cemetery.

"Though the fact of the matter is that you're not big at all; you're still a little boy and the reason for all your troubles is that you're still living like a little boy in the world of prohibitions. I'm referring, of course, to the issue of carnal tribulations that is so fundamental for you. As far back as you can remember, you lived under an absolute taboo on carnality. When you were a very young boy, a child still, and you began to take a lively interest in such things, they were forbidden to you, because as everyone knows such things are forbidden to young boys—"

"Are you sure," Kohoutek interrupted her, "that a cemetery is the right place for this sort of conversation?"

"O foolish Kohoutek," said Kohoutek's good-looking wife, without in the least altering her mild tone, "O foolish Kohoutek, you who have been known to have eight hundred women in a single weekend; you don't have the faintest idea either about women or about the world. If you knew, Kohoutek, how many women have lost their virginity in the cemeteries of the world, your spiritual life would not be so impoverished. A cemetery is a good and tranquil spot; those who lie here are at peace with the world and our temporary wantonness won't disturb their rest. Kohoutek," she continued, "you eternal seeker of safe places, of secluded benches in parks, out-of-the-way groves, deserted alleys, darkened gateways, suburban woods; you unwearying invader of unoccupied gazebos, allotment gardens, and riverside bushes; has it never occurred to you to take one of your numerous girlfriends to a cemetery, to take her on a romantic walk to the garden of the dead, perfumed with flowers and filled with sultry July air?"

This had in fact never occurred to Kohoutek, but before he had time to reply, his doleful child suddenly perked up and shouted, "Look! Look! A stag!"

At the top of the cemetery, among the crosses, a female deer was grazing calmly in the tall white grass.

"It's a doe, honey," said Kohoutek. The animal raised its head, disturbed by the child's cry; for a moment it stared in their direction, then set off uphill at a stately pace and soon disappeared among the trunks of the birch trees that grew there.

"You see, Kohoutek, even the creatures of the forest know this place is safe. No one will shoot at them here. The dead sportsmen aren't going to rise up from their graves to organize a hunting party. The grass growing from the remains of our Protestant ancestors is as fertile and invigorating as the ideas of the Reformation. A cemetery is a good and tranquil spot, while love and death are close to one another. You know that much yourself, Kohoutek; they taught that even at schools under the Muscovite yoke."

"Yes, that much I know," said Kohoutek sarcastically and strained to recall some of the details, clearly without much success.

"Since you know, you'll allow me to tell you what I have to say. Besides, I have to do it here and now, because at other times and in other places I don't have the opportunity. At home your mother takes part in all our conversations; we don't often go to cafés or on walks, on the whole we spend our evenings and our nights apart, and you're often away. . . . Though recently you've been going away a little less often; could it be that you've found something local, or maybe someone's come here?"

"All right, say what you have to say"—a certain irritation could be heard in Kohoutek's voice—"and get on with it."

"But what I have to say will be very short, no more than a few sentences." Kohoutek's wife looked once more toward the top of the cemetery, where their doleful child was wandering among the birches.

"So you-know-what was always prohibited to you," she began again. "When you were a young boy even your own body was forbidden. And so you constantly had to hide, desperately taking your interests underground, seeing yourself on the quiet, secretly studying the usual literature, contemplating the usual pictures with a constant feeling of danger. Your later childhood and the stormy years of adolescence passed in this way. Unfortunately, very early on, much too early on, at the age of barely seventeen you met me, a woman also of seventeen. You soon realized that I didn't belong to the opponent's camp, among the dismal company of those who per- petually withheld from you access to the forbidden fruit. . . . Quite the opposite, I let you do everything, and sometimes I even encouraged you to do everything, because you were a nice boy who smelled good, Kohoutek. And so it might have seemed that the times of constraint, of fear and endless conspiracies, were over for good. Nothing could have been more mistaken. We were still chil- dren"—Kohoutek's wife took his arm gently—"and we still had to hide. Now there was a double prohibition, which had spread from you to me, and in a certain sense it had grown even more burden- some. Before, you only hid your own filthy thoughts, your books, maybe some dirty pictures. Now the two of us both had to hide ourselves away; we had to hide from the world our two bodies clinging to each other. Conspiracy in theory is a lot easier than conspiracy in practice. What's more, Kohoutek, I began to desert you. I began gradually crossing over to the camp of your ancient en- emies; I gradually began to forbid things to you, to restrain you. I tracked your thoughts as they turned toward women other than me, persecuted those glances of yours that were directed the wrong way, and crushed the hopes you entertained of trying to meet anyone besides me. I soon became your strictest jailer; I forbade you absolutely everything other than myself, while as far as I myself was concerned, Kohoutek, as you well know, I also didn't allow you to do just anything—certain things were absolutely prohibited, and certain of your desires could never be fulfilled since they had been forbidden to you once and for all. Moreover, while I was your strictest jailer, we were both still subject to general prohibitions; we were dogged by our parents, my envious girlfriends, your dumb buddies, receptionists in hotels, the owners of guest houses, porters, everyone. When we got married the situation didn't improve much. We didn't have a place of our own; to begin with we were cooped up in my folks' two-room apartment, where I didn't think about love so much as about the excessively creaky bed; then we moved in here, where first of all it's not much better, and second it's already too late. For some time already you, Kohoutek, had begun to break away desperately; you'd begun to look for a love which if not entirely then certainly to a significant degree would not be forbidden. And you discovered that the only truly permissible love is the love that is completely forbidden by everyone. Because a condition of real forbidden love is its admittedly temporary and yet absolute safety. You're experienced in these things and you know that above all a person needs to find a good, safe place, like this cemetery. A place where for an hour at least, for a single evening, there are no prohibitions. And that was how you decided to live: in a perpetual series of on-off enchantments. This is the source of your lack of restraint: You sin, break prohibitions, and expose yourself to endless dangers so that for a moment you can feel sinless, free, and safe. Your tragedy is that at such moments you genuinely believe that you *are* sinless, free, and safe. From your real torments of the flesh, from the fact that as the apostle Paul says you 'suffer eternal fire,' you, Kohoutek, draw false intellectual conclusions. You understand my meaning?"

They stopped in front of a grave that had been carefully deco-
rated with fir branches. In the center lay a wreath of wildflowers
that Oma had made two weeks before. The plain granite headstone
carried the inscription "Emilian Kohoutek, Master Butcher,
1869–1956." Kohoutek's wife reached down and placed the rose
across the wreath. She put her hands together as if to say a prayer
and repeated, "You understand my meaning?"

"No," replied Kohoutek.

"Very well, I'll explain it to you in a minute. For now, think
about your great-grandfather."

Kohoutek often thought about his great-grandfather. He didn't
remember him at all. We old chroniclers of that epoch remember
him perfectly. Emilian Kohoutek lived a stormy and roisterous life
till the end of his days. He traveled. Perpetually at odds with the
other inhabitants of the house, at least once a month he would
move out permanently. When he came back, as if to mark the temporary nature of his return, he would always take up residence in
the furthest room, which was never heated. There was nothing in
it but an iron bed and a massive carboy full of wine he had made
from whatever fruit was available.

Till the very end he believed that the old slaughterhouse would
operate at full steam once again under his command. He wouldn't
agree to the sale of the slowly deteriorating machinery. He was forever traveling to Cieszyn with fantastical plans for administrative
procedures that would supposedly lead to the reopening of the establishment. Out of respect for his venerable age and probably also
out of fear of his irascibility, the municipal clerks omitted to remind
him that before the war his butcher's business had already been
hugely in debt and virtually bankrupt. After each unsuccessful expedition to the district authorities he would return drunk as a skunk.

Kohoutek always subconsciously imagined that his great-grand-father was the spitting image of Dr. Oyermah. It's possible that there were certain inner similarities between them. But physically old Kohoutek was the complete reverse of Oyermah. He was a short, slightly built man with a particularly characteristic parting and, it might be said, an even more characteristic short mustache. During the occupation his astonishing resemblance to the dictator frequently smoothed his way and probably saved his life. In the scrupulous copy of their leader's mustache and hairstyle the naive invaders perceived an expression of sincere homage. On the contrary, it was Emilian Kohoutek the master butcher who regarded the führer as a paltry imitator and primarily for that reason held him in utter contempt.

He died as he had lived, in violation of universally accepted mores. He passed away in the very heart of a freezing, snowbound winter. Though he himself had been of abject height and inferior build, the casket in which they placed him was immense and heavy like everything in those times. When, just as the funeral cortege was about to turn off the main avenue of the cemetery toward the open grave, the casket slipped from the hands of the pallbearers and crashed to the ground, no one was really surprised. It had rather been expected that something like this would happen; in fact, truth to tell, all the many people attending the funeral were quietly hoping that old Kohoutek would let his presence be felt one more time before he was laid to rest. Yet no one anticipated the panache with which he would do so. For along with the coffin, the son of the deceased, the postmaster, Kohoutek's grandfather, also tumbled to the ground. He fell in such an unfortunate way that he knocked his head against the front of the coffin, which started to slide down the ice-covered gravel. In essence it was an impressive soccer play: Flinging himself almost at ground level, with a flying header the son had tapped the casket containing his father and had set it on a distant course. The stunned mourners stepped aside as the coffin glided past their feet. It was said later that they didn't so much step aside as scatter in panic, because as the casket bounced over the frozen stones it gave out such a terrifying clatter that everyone had the impression old Kohoutek had risen from the dead, woken up, and with his usual impulsiveness was trying to get out. And everyone watched mutely as the ghastly conveyance rushed downhill, picking up speed and heading in the exact direction of Helena Morcinkówna (trumpet) as she climbed the cemetery avenue.

That's right. Little Helena Morcinkówna, who at the beginning of the century had been the second to appear on the stage at the Hart Inn in Cieszyn and had played the trumpet, was trailing along behind the funeral procession. All her life she had been mortally and unhappily in love with Emilian. He cared nothing for her love; he despised it and mocked it. He had had other women—which, by the way, he was not accustomed to concealing, even from his own wife, who was just as unhappy as Helena, if not more so. Helena thought about him all her life. It never occurred to her to meet someone else, though he never met with her. It never occurred to her to talk to someone else, though he never talked to her. She never thought about dancing with someone else, though he had never asked her to dance. She never thought that someone else could come to her lonely house, though he never came. She waited. And the longer she waited, the more firmly she believed that the moment would come. So now, when she heard the rumble and saw the coffin sliding down toward her, she knew beyond a doubt: Her darling, having crossed the threshold of the other world, had finally understood her love and was hurrying to meet her. And little Helena Morcinkówna flung aside the walking stick she was leaning on and spread her arms. The rapidly moving casket threw her frail legs up and she crashed onto the lid. She gripped the wooden case with all her strength as it continued to gather speed under her weight, shot through the open cemetery gate, and began to hurtle down the narrow path that led to the river. It looked as if some unseen hand was indeed guiding the coffin, or as if Helena herself, like a seasoned bobsledder, was taking the successive curves and turns. Finally, at the steep bank of the river came the finishing line—the late Kohoutek and his finally happy woman sped down onto the frozen surface, and for a long time the coffin continued to travel down the river like a boat bearing newlyweds. It really did seem as if Emilian Kohoutek had decided to escape the grave, to take Helena, and to set off with her on a primitive raft made only of a few boards nailed together toward warm seas and the Happy Islands.

Kohoutek had often heard the unbelievable story of his great-grandfather's funeral, but he always imagined that he had witnessed it himself. "Maybe I once dreamed about that casket sliding down the steep slope; maybe I saw a similar scene in some movie; maybe it's described somewhere in a book." Kohoutek remembers his current woman; his good-looking and well-educated wife is on his arm, while with his other hand he leads his gloomy child, and they all walk slowly down the same gravel path along which, many years before, the master butcher Emilian Kohoutek had taken his immortal coffin-bound sleigh ride.

15

"Brothers and sisters who are drowning in drink!" thundered the pastor. "Drunkards and sots! You who are not drowning, you who have drowned already—I speak to you today!"

After writing a sermon, the pastor would always read it aloud. That is, he would not so much read it as deliver it with his old preacher's gusto, with the old, somewhat exaggerated theatrical inflections. He had retired two years before and now only rarely entered the pulpit; yet he continued his former practice of writing a sermon every week, and, as if practicing for a real service, he would perform it in his study. Recently he had been doing so more frequently. The homiletic muse descended upon him at the oddest times of the day or week. It sometimes happened that in the middle of dinner, between the first and second course, he would jump up from the table, run to his room, and slam the door; then three or four hours later his sonorous voice would begin to issue forth from inside.

When a sermon was beginning, the inhabitants of the house stopped whatever they were doing, took a seat in the kitchen, and listened. After all, there was no way they could ignore the word of God ringing through every room. Though there was no denying that the more often the pastor began his sermons and the stranger the times, the more onerous it became. Now too, when Kohoutek heard the eternal invocation "Brothers and sisters," he could have screamed. His mother and the pastor's wife were just setting off for the church hall for Bible study and it was a fine opportunity to go by the attic of the old slaughterhouse, and here he had to listen to the pastor admonishing drunks.

"It is only now that are you beginning to understand," his voice could be heard, "the awful meaning of the phrase 'drowning one's sorrows and cares in alcohol,' or, as the idiomatic expression has it, 'hitting the bottle.' It is only now that you comprehend the true meaning of this phrase; and yet how banal and trite it once seemed to you!"

In a wordless rage, Kohoutek's mother and the pastor's wife removed the overcoats they had already put on and made their way to the kitchen; they were followed by Kohoutek, who was followed by Miss Wandzia and her mother; then came Kohoutek's good-looking wife with a foreign-language textbook. Oma and the postmaster were already seated at the table. Finally there appeared Kohoutek's doleful child wearing a Walkman. When Kohoutek's mother saw him she stared in a stern and disciplinary manner at his covered ears; but the child not only did not yield but returned the stare with a gaze so profoundly lugubrious that Kohoutek's mother capitulated and turned away. Everyone sat, silent and, with the exception of Oma, pale with fury, and listened to the sermon.

"Yes, now that your drowsy heads are bent over a full glass like the surface of a lake," the voice stormed from the depths of the house, "now that the glass is so immense that in order to look upon it you must raise your drowsy heads, and even so you cannot see its top, for it is hidden by clouds; now you understand what it means to 'drown in booze,' what it means to be 'at the bottom of the glass.'

To you I speak, frequenters of saloons! To you I speak, you who are sitting in the bar! Yet you imagine, brothers and sisters, that those who look upon you see you as you see yourselves. You imagine that they see a man or a woman, sedate and mature in years, who, wielding the familiar vessel in hand, is taking a little sip of the invigorating nectar; you imagine that those who look upon you think that you wish to rest after arduous labor or to calm your shaken nerves, or to gather your thoughts before taking an important decision. How mistaken you are; how you are misled by your booze-addled senses! What you take for reality is such a nebulous hallucination that one cannot but laugh. Ha ha ha ha ha!" the pastor laughed, or rather pretended to laugh a truly Frankensteinesque laugh, and Kohoutek's flesh crept. "What sedate and mature man! A boy! A dwarf! A midget! A pygmy! What sedate and mature woman! A child! A suckling! A dwarf woman! Little Red Riding Hood! And there is no familiar vessel that you are wielding in your hand. That vessel is unfamiliar, unknown, and unheard of. It is as huge as a glass mountain. As an Olympic swimming pool. As the great globe of the earth. It may be that someone else's fingers are wielding that vessel. But not your fingers. You are a scrap floating upon the depths. You, wretched drunkard, are like a tiny homunculus swimming in an ever-clumsier breaststroke upon the depths. Here there's no person with a glass in their hand; there's only a glass with a person at its bottom! There's no bar! There's no saloon! There's only a cabinet of curiosities filled with glass jars in which your tiny skeletons are floating. There's only a gallery of aquaria—what am I saying, a gallery of alcoholaria—here in fine cognac"—the pastor's voice acquired an unexpected warmth—"a fashionable gent in a suit is swimming about like a guppy; he's coping well so far, swimming jauntily from one end of the tank to the other. Here in the greenish waters of Bison Brand vodka, a woman beautiful as a fantail goldfish is clearly summoning the last of her strength; here, in red wine, a scientist like a goodeid is at the point of death, and no one will learn anything rational from him ever again." The pastor was speaking with ever-greater cordiality, tenderness even. "Here one who is virtually a child is splashing about like a million fish in champagne, and it will be the last bath that the poor creature takes in its life; here a father and a family man, a venerable black moor, is acting like a youngster and frolicking about in digestive bitters. . . ."

A moment of silence followed. The pastor was probably crossing something out in the text of the sermon. It's strange, thought Kohoutek, how people know so much. For instance, how did the pastor come to be such an expert on alcohol and on keeping aquarium fish? It's strange, though not that strange, he reflected a moment later, because after all you could just ask someone about which fish are kept in an aquarium; you could ask someone who has an aquarium. Kohoutek had solved yet another of the mysteries of his life and felt an immeasurable sense of relief.

"Brothers and sisters! Drunkards! Sots! Topers!" the pastor continued. "Even if you imagine you have traveled the whole world, you are mistaken; you have been nowhere, for booze obliterates space. You have not been in the north; at most you have been in a northern bar. You have not been in the south—you were in a southern bar. You were in an eastern bar and a western bar. But you were neither in the east nor in the west. You have not been in warm countries, but only in their bars. The bars of the world are all the same, and so you went around the world yet in reality you stayed where you were. For you there is no space and for you there is no time; for one who is drowning in a glass, time ceases to exist. You see him!" the pastor cried abruptly, and everyone thought that the pastor must have actually noticed a physical person; but it was merely a striking rhetorical ploy. "You see him! The fallen drunk! He raises his glass. Does he ask the time? A day goes by and it seems to him that a second has gone by. A month goes by and it seems to him that a minute has gone by. A year goes by and he thinks an hour has passed. He is invulnerable to time! No, time crushes him! For he believes that only a few hours have passed, yet half his life is over. And do not hide booze within yourself, brother, do not conceal it in your sickly innards. You will hide nothing. While she, your sister booze, sooner or later will begin to emerge from you.

"Brothers and sisters!" Among those sitting at the table a certain easing of tension could be felt, since the pastor's tone indicated that he was drawing to a close.

"Brothers and sisters! The apostle Paul tells you not to keep with the licentious of this world, not to keep with drunkards and not to eat with them. Yet how can you not eat with drunkards since you are drunkards yourselves? In that case you cannot eat with yourselves, and what is more, you no longer do eat with yourselves. You do not eat with yourselves because you are not yourselves. Therefore do as the apostle instructs: Remove that spitfire from your midst. Amen."

Kohoutek placed his hands together in prayer. "Lord," he whispered, "there's some sensual spitfire sitting inside me, while on the outside I'm surrounded by a close circle of all-knowing and incessantly speechifying men, and of women gifted with a devilish intuition. Lord, I'm not taking your name in vain, but things can't go on like this."

16

"Oma was here. She was complaining about all of you." Kohoutek's current woman looked at him reproachfully. "She complained that your father pays no attention to her and treats her as if she wasn't there. She complained that your mother won't let her eat what she wants to. She said that in his sermons the pastor's always reproving her for overeating and overdrinking. She complained that Miss Wandzia's daughter plays the violin too quietly, because she'd be glad to listen to some music from time to time. That poor, poor old lady." Tears appeared in Kohoutek's current woman's eyes. "Oma also said that the pastor's wife ought not to cut her hair under any circumstances and that Miss Wandzia ought not to force her daughter to play the violin since the girl doesn't want to. She resented the fact that your wife," said Kohoutek's current woman pointedly, "is forever sitting with her nose in books, and foreign ones at that; if they weren't foreign books she might at least be able to read to her from time to time. And last of all she held it against her husband, the postmaster, that he doesn't protect her from all of you."

Despite the state of dismay in which he found himself, Kohoutek experienced the classic unsatisfied need of the person who has been overlooked.

"She didn't have any complaints about me?" he asked.

"Not really," said his current woman with a certain hesitation in her voice. "Not really. . . . She just mentioned that she's afraid. . . ."

"Afraid of what?"

"She's a little afraid that one of these days you'll marry a Catholic."

The circle is closing in, thought Kohoutek in despair.

"It may be that the old lady has certain details wrong, but when it comes down to it this isn't about details." Kohoutek's current woman was speaking rapidly and decisively now. "Besides, Oma didn't ask me if I was Catholic. I was the only one she had no complaints about whatsoever," she added with sudden triumph in her voice. "She thanked me and she complimented me," continued Kohoutek's current woman. "I helped her climb upstairs, and she said it was a long time since anyone had helped her up any stairs. I gave her some tea from the thermos, and she said she couldn't remember the last time anybody had made tea for her. She brought me some kolach and she told me that before long she'd bring some yeast babka."

"She wasn't surprised that you're living here?" Kohoutek sensed that his simple and rational question was in the present situation merely absurd and bothersome.

"Of course not! She only asked if I wasn't cold. She said that in the furthest room there's an unused iron bed with a good straw mattress and a great big eiderdown, and that you should bring it all here, because there'll be frosts any day now. She also asked me (though she apologized for the question, and I'm sure I blushed when I answered), she also asked me where I go to the bathroom. . . ."

"Right," murmured Kohoutek.

"I showed her, and she said it would be better to use a potty, and that there's a potty in the laundry room, and that you know exactly which potty she means, because it used to be your potty."

"Fine," said Kohoutek, "I'll bring you my potty."

"And the bed, and the mattress, and the eiderdown."

"Right," said Kohoutek quietly, "I'll bring you the bed, and the mattress, and the eiderdown."

"You see, Kohoutek"—his current woman touched his hand—"when you want, you can be wonderful."

For a moment she sat good humored and smiling, then she said, "Next week I'll go to the local school and ask if they don't need a Polish teacher. I ought to start looking around for work soon. I wouldn't want to be a burden on you."

"Aha. That's great," replied Kohoutek. "That's a great idea."

"Kohoutek"—Kohoutek's current woman was in an exceptionally cheery mood; Oma's astounding visit seemed to have given her untold inner strength—"Kohoutek, do you remember how we met?"

"Sure I remember," Kohoutek replied automatically. "We met on the A line express bus. You were reading a book and I sat in front of you and asked you what you were reading."

"Do you remember what I replied?"

"Yes, I remember; you said you were reading Kundera."

"But at that time, Kohoutek," said Kohoutek's current woman gently, "you didn't know if Kundera was the name of the author or the title of the book; you didn't know, did you?"

Kohoutek grew irritated.

"I didn't know then," he said, raising his voice, "and as a matter of fact I still don't know now. I haven't a clue when it comes to books; I know nothing about prose, and as far as poetry is concerned, I don't understand a thing. As far as poetry is concerned," he repeated distinctly, looking her directly in the eye, "I don't understand a single comma."

His current woman shrank into herself and lowered her head. It seemed that the good mood had dissipated completely.

◈ ◈ ◈

Once in her apartment in Kraków, when they had been getting ready to eat supper and she, as usual, had been tidying the table strewn with books and papers, a loose white sheet of paper had fallen to the floor. Kohoutek picked it up without thinking and turned it over in his hands. On the other side were a few lines in her handwriting. It was a poem bearing the title, incomprehensible to Kohoutek, of "Haiku":

Notebooks filled with mysterious writings
Grass of ink
over a vast expanse
Someone is walking through darkness
Someone is furious

Kohoutek read this work through once and then a second time, and despite the fact that inwardly he felt a growing sense of bewilderment, he asked no questions. He did nothing whatsoever. And above all he did nothing bad. He didn't laugh in that high-pitched, disagreeable giggle of his, nor did he shape his features into an expression of derision. He stood motionless, and it was certain that not one of his accidental and insignificant gestures was a gesture directed against poetry. Nevertheless, she threw herself upon him with the ferocity of a painfully uncovered lyrical subject, grabbing the paper from his hand, tearing it up, and glowering at him with the most murderous look in her repertoire. From that moment the inscrutable five-line haiku grew between them like an unscalable wall. They never spoke of it; he had no idea whether it was her only poem or one of thousands she had written; he didn't dare to ask, while she gave no explanations. Only from time to time, when he felt particularly hurt by her, would he make the effort to utter a venomous allusion and emphasize that he knew nothing, absolutely nothing about poetry.

❖ ❖ ❖

Yet this time, after a moment of silence Kohoutek's current woman decided to pretend that his ritual gibe had passed her by. "That's right, I was reading a samizdat edition of Milan Kundera's *The Book of Laughter and Forgetting.* Kohoutek, I have that book with me; allow me to read you an excerpt." And Kohoutek's current woman took from her suitcase a tattered volume bound in newspaper and began to read "Petrarch's Story." We old admirers of the Czech author know that excerpt well. It is the moment when the country's most eminent poets meet in the Prague writers' club. Kundera gives them the names of the great authors of world literature. Thus, there is Goethe (an elderly poet walking with difficulty on crutches); there is Voltaire, Lermontov, Yesenin, and Boccaccio. And there is Petrarch, whose story Kohoutek's current woman is reading to him at this time. Petrarch tells the tale of an unexpected visit paid him late one evening by a certain young female poet. Let us add to be clear: The young poet was not Petrarch's current woman. Nevertheless, Petrarch cannot receive her, since his beautiful and jealous wife is at home, while the young poet is behaving mysteriously and unpredictably. She won't come at another time, but she won't leave either. She doesn't allow herself to be sent away. "There's something I have to tell you, there's something I have to tell you," she keeps repeating. For a long time she stands at the door, then finally she breaks Petrarch's windows with an iron bar; she enters his house through the last broken window and says to him, "I came because I was driven here by love; I came so you could know what true love is, so you could experience it at least once in your life."

And then the girl takes Petrarch's beautiful wife by the hand and says, "You're not angry with me, because you're a good person and I love you too, I love you both."

◈ ◈ ◈

Kohoutek's current woman read the excerpt to the end, and the moment she had finished Kohoutek, recklessly and with his characteristic literary simplemindedness, asked, "So do you mean to break the windows in my house with an iron bar?"

His current woman looked up at him with her beautiful eyes, whose color now was reminiscent of a frozen river (down which an oaken casket was gliding), and she said, "O naive Kohoutek. A person breaks windows with a iron bar in the house of a Petrarch or a Kundera, or the greatest Polish writer, about whom you are decidedly unplatonically jealous, you're brutishly jealous and you are entirely right to be. In your house, Kohoutek, a person doesn't break windows. A person comes to your house to stay there forever."

"I'm treating myself with booze and aspirin, my dear Kohoutek; though I won't conceal from you the fact that I sometimes forget to take the aspirin."

Oyermah was sitting in an armchair; his sheepskin was thrown directly over his pajamas and he looked poorly. His features were drawn, and several days' gray stubble aged him mightily; truth be told, Kohoutek looked at him for the first time with a certain apprehension.

"Perhaps we should call a doctor," he said hesitantly.

"Kohoutek, would you be so kind as to light the stove and not sap every last ounce of my strength with suggestions of that kind? You know perfectly well that you and I are both just as much doctors as those experts in human ailments. I've told you a thousand times that there is virtually no difference between a human being and an animal. As is written in Ecclesiastes—." Here Oyermah was beset by such a ferocious coughing fit that it seemed he would be unable to repeat his favorite quotation for the thousand and first time. But that moment had not yet come. He calmed down, took a long draught of clear liquid from a glass that stood by his armchair, raised his hand and in his usual resonant voice said, "As is written in Ecclesiastes: 'For that which befalleth the sons of men befalleth beasts; even one thing befalleth them: as the one dieth, so dieth the other; yea, they all have one breath; so that a man hath no preeminence over a beast: for all is vanity.' And further it is written: 'Who knoweth the spirit of man that goeth upward, and the spirit of the beast that goeth downward to the earth?'"

"You know, master," said Kohoutek as he cleaned the ash from the great tiled stove, "I sometimes think that we Lutherans are marked by an excessive and somewhat impunitive facility in the way we continually cite the Scriptures. Besides, to be honest it's easy to lose sight of who we really are—wise men, shepherds, or cattle?"

Oyermah waved his hand impatiently.

"I don't like those kinds of generalizations. The fact that I, Franciszek Józef Oyermah, know the Scriptures and cite them doesn't mean that our fellow worshipers also knew the Scriptures. The old Protestants did indeed know the Bible; but all the old Protestants apart from me are dead. Time was! But today?" The doctor grew despondent. "One of the most painful circumstances of my life is the fact that just before my death I have to look on helplessly as the Lutheran Church is taken over by pathetic holier-than-thou women and theological morons such as, with all due respect, yourself, Kohoutek."

Kohoutek said nothing, hurt, while Oyermah, guessing that he was sore, as usual declaimed with paternal severity, "You've no reason to take offense. After all it was you, in your typically muddleheaded fashion incidentally, who recently presented to me a theory according to which the only way of drawing close to the countenance of the Lord is by breaking the Sixth Commandment. By the way, how is the situation?"

"It's become aggravated," replied Kohoutek and told Oyermah about Oma's astonishing visit to the attic of the old slaughterhouse, about his current woman's growing desire to stay for good, and also about the conversation he had had with his good-looking wife, who, though vaguely and indirectly, nevertheless gave him to understand that she would take steps. . . .

"Surely you're not surprised at her," said Oyermah tartly. "Surely you don't think that such a beautiful and well-educated woman will endure at your side. She'll neither endure nor will she fulfill your expectations. You shouldn't have married such a wise and good-looking woman. True love, Kohoutek, should be sought among sickly hunchbacks, infirm females in glasses, and slow-witted orphan girls."

"When she married me she was neither that beautiful nor that bright. Beauty and wisdom came to her with age," retorted Kohoutek.

"True," murmured Oyermah. "As usual, you ended up with the most difficult case."

Kohoutek was attempting in vain to light the fire he had prepared. The blue-tiled stove was cold, and clouds of smoke were filling the room.

"Open the window." Oyermah covered himself tightly with his sheepskin. "Open the window; there's no better smell than the smell of icy autumn air mixed with the smell of the first smoke from a slowly warming stove.

"But the fact of the matter is, Kohoutek, that you have a fatal fondness in general," continued the doctor, "for good-looking and well-educated women. We need look no further than the person who is the subject of our discussion, the one it's not clear what should be done with, the one who paid you an unannounced visit"—Oyermah laughed in amusement at his own thought—"the one who paid you an unannounced visit, exactly like our Bolshevik leaders were wont to do in times past."

"They used to visit workplaces unexpectedly, but only for a short time," said Kohoutek, clearly displeased by the comparison.

"Fine. I only want to say that she transgresses exceedingly on the side of beauty, or rather of a peculiar charm. Those slightly asymmetrical features, that divine outline of her skull, that stupendous hairstyle. . . . Observe, Kohoutek, that your current woman has taken her hair, which is basically typical for the average auburn-haired woman, and has managed to style it in an alarmingly decadent fashion. Oh," gushed Oyermah, "that slight squint of hers, those slightly knock-kneed legs. . . ."

"How exactly do you know that she's knock-kneed?" Kohoutek suddenly straightened up; the first pale flames began to flicker in the stove.

"A woman with such a unique countenance has to be slightly knock-kneed," Oyermah retorted categorically. And he added, "Besides, it's all the same what kind of knees she has; what interests us are the reasons why she chose to traipse all the way to your house on those slightly or maybe even more than slightly knock-kneed legs (toting a suitcase full of books and a backpack with the rest of her belongings), with the intention of staying for good."

To Kohoutek's utter astonishment Oyermah took from his pocket a sheet of paper torn from an exercise book and folded in four, opened it, reached for his eyeglasses, and intently studied the notes written on it.

Oh no, thought Kohoutek, oh no; the old guy's prepared notes for his speech. Oh no. I'll never get out of here.

All at once the sheet of paper in Oyermah's hands began to tremble; he himself gave a heavy sigh and then another, and fat beads of perspiration appeared on his forehead. With a curiously slow and helpless gesture the doctor put the notes on his lap, removed his glasses, and wiped the sweat from his forehead with the collar of his pajama top.

"I'm in a bad way, Kohoutek," he said softly. "A very bad way. It'll be hard for me to leave you, believe me, it'll be hard, but you have to reckon with that possibility." He reached for the glass and, holding it in two suddenly weakened hands, raised it to his lips.

"Master," asked Kohoutek mildly, "are you sure that's the right medicine?"

"When your time comes, there's no right or wrong medicine." Oyermah drank a considerable portion of the drink that was in the glass. "And my time is coming; in fact, it's already here. Last night I dreamed of Akiko again. Whenever I dream of that Asian bitch, nothing good comes of it. And recently I've been dreaming of her every night, all night long. Like your current woman, she refuses to abandon the man of her life." Oyermah evidently felt better again.

"Coming back to the subject in hand," he said, this time, it seemed, in a rather artificially animated voice. He picked up the sheet of paper again, again put on his glasses, and like a seasoned lecturer he began to expound upon the problem.

"The possible reasons why your current woman did what she did are numerous, and as follows. She may have done it because she wished to force you to take a definitive decision, to say yes or no, to assume an actual position. In such a case her arrival would be blackmail, or at any rate a kind of blackmail. She may have been brought here by a mad feminine love, or perhaps feminine cruelty. She may have come not of her own free will"—Oyermah was speaking with the utmost seriousness—"but rather was led here by the same demon who once sent a yellow Volga for the two of you. What demon was it? Who knows? The demon of blackmail? The demon of love? The demon of cruelty? Or perhaps everything is actually much simpler; maybe she decided to pay you an unannounced visit because she's just an ordinary unpredictable young lady?"

"Either she's ordinary, or she's unpredictable," said Kohoutek.

"Among the younger generations there are so many unpredictable young ladies that they constitute the ordinary majority. That's how it seems to an old fogy like me." For a minute Oyermah stared at the flames blazing away briskly; the windows were closed now and the room was growing warmer.

"What's her field?" he asked after a moment. "Polish?"

"Yes, this year she graduated in Polish literature," said Kohoutek hesitantly, since the fact of the matter was that as far as his current woman was concerned he wasn't entirely sure of anything.

"She's from Kraków?"

"No. In Kraków she has—she had," Kohoutek corrected himself sarcastically, "a room. But she's originally from Ostrowiec Świętokrzyski. From Ostrowiec itself or somewhere nearby—I'm not certain."

"If I might ask," Oyermah continued his interrogation, "what is the name of your femme fatale from Ostrowiec Świętokrzyski?"

"Kotkowska. Justyna Kotkowska."

Oyermah fell deep in thought; it might even have seemed as if he had collapsed inwardly, that he had had another weak spell; but he was merely thinking feverishly, trying to recall something. Outside it was slowly turning dark. The eternal fire was roaring in the blue stove.

Oyermah looked at Kohoutek intently, and even with a certain tension.

"Listen, she hasn't by any chance said anything to you about being related by blood or by marriage to Gombrowicz?"

"Actually yes, she once mentioned that if she really tried, she could show that they were relatives." Kohoutek hesitated. "In any case, that name came up at the time."

"The situation is becoming grave," muttered Oyermah.

Once again he fell silent, raised his head, and for a while stared at the reproduction of *The Last Supper* hanging on the wall.

"The situation is becoming grave," he repeated. "If your current woman considers herself to be Gombrowicz's cousin, the situation is grave; but I categorically reject the hypothesis that when she came here to you she was led by some obscure literary motive. I reject that hypothesis"—Oyermah was speaking in a tone of casual nonchalance which he hardly ever employed—"I reject it, because it solves nothing. Just as I reject the notion, which has long been going around in your mind, that she is a divine punishment brought upon you for your transgressions. I know that that pathetic idea has been gnawing at you since the very beginning, but you're embarrassed to talk about it with me, and rightly so."

Fine, Kohoutek whispered to himself in his soul, fine, you old buffoon, you know everything about me, but I know a thing or two about you as well. Right now you'll deliver a great tirade about feminine cruelty, and then for the hundredth time you'll tell me the story of Akiko.

"I hope," said Oyermah, "that you can guess what my opinion is. It is this: In my opinion, she was driven to come to you by ordinary feminine cruelty. Unfortunately, I don't have the strength"— Oyermah finished up what was left of the liquor in the glass—"I don't have the strength to remind you of my theory concerning the cruelty of women. I'll just tell you the story of Akiko. But before I begin I'd like to ask you to be so kind as to do the following: Make some tea for me; make some for yourself too of course; pour me some more booze; pour yourself some too of course—the bottle's in the dresser—and bring me two aspirins from the medicine cabinet."

18

"As you know, Kohoutek, this story takes place just before the outbreak of the Second World War in the Luisendorf guest house in London. It features three people: a beautiful young Japanese woman called Akiko, a certain odious British essayist with a fiery gaze, and myself, Franciszek Józef Oyermah. It's a torrid summer; I spend the days honing my theoretical knowledge and learning the language, while in the evenings I suffer the torments of hotel solitude. In the room opposite mine—"

"Excuse me, master," said Kohoutek, "but I believe there's someone knocking at the door."

Oyermah fell silent and after a moment a delicate tapping was indeed heard.

"Kohoutek, go and see if my darling Józefina is already here for me, or the Grim Reaper himself, or some other representative of darkness; tell them that my last wish is to tell the story of Akiko one more time. . . ."

"I think, Doctor, it's more the case that life itself has appeared in its inscrutable form. . . ."

"Oh, I see." Oyermah caught on immediately. "How did she find her way here?"

"She knows the whole town like the back of her hand from my tales. I'm in the insufferably sentimental habit of telling my current women all about the Cieszyn region."

"Very well. Intellectually speaking your situation is irresolvable anyway, so further inquiry would be pointless. At most I'll simply give you both a certain practical piece of advice and I'll also finish the story of Akiko, in the censored version due to the presence of a lady. Invite her in while I get dressed."

Kohoutek's current woman was wearing the navy-blue overcoat in which she had arrived, and her divine skull was covered by the funky little hat. She entered the room and with an importunate curiosity stared at the huge sofa, the Pionier radio next to it, the armchair with the brownish-green upholstery, the upright piano, the tiled stove whose little door was growing red hot, and at the table that stood in the middle of the room and was covered with a yellow tablecloth. She went up to the window and looked out at the lights twinkling in the darkness.

"I like it here," she murmured, "I like it here more and more."

That's right, thought Kohoutek, she didn't come here because of me; she came here because this is a scenically attractive location. She likes it here. She wants to spend the rest of her life here. Yesterday she met Oma, in a moment she'll meet Oyermah, and one by one she'll meet other adherents of the Lutheran faith. It may be that she'll meet my other friends and relatives. She'll take a job in the school. She'll find herself an apartment. In the long run it's not inconceivable that she'll come and live with me. And she'll no longer be my current woman. Maybe she no longer is already.

The room filled with the oppressive fragrance of Wars cologne. Dr. Franciszek Józef Oyermah stood in the doorway. He had shaved and had combed his hair meticulously. He had donned black pants, a light blue shirt, and a jacket of thick brownish-yellow tweed. Around his neck he had tied a claret-colored cravat.

115

"The clown," Kohoutek whispered to himself. "The old clown." But when he looked more closely at Oyermah a moment later, for the second time that evening he was seriously dismayed. It was clear that the change of outfit and the perfunctory grooming (though it had been carried out at astonishing speed) were actions that surpassed the old man's strength. White as a sheet, he was breathing heavily, or rather spasmodically opening his mouth, trying in vain to take a deep breath. He staggered and grabbed hold of the door frame. They ran up to him, took him by the arms, and led him to the armchair. Kohoutek's current woman took off her overcoat and with extraordinary diligence and solicitude took care of Oyermah, though in one sense all her actions—loosening his cravat, wiping the perspiration from his brow, checking his pulse—were in vain, since as soon as Oyermah managed to catch his breath he decided to celebrate the fact by taking another mouthful of booze, after which, naturally, he felt much better.

"I apologize," he said composedly, "for my less than successful entrée."

"I'm the one who should apologize for intruding on you unexpectedly; though, as you know, Doctor, unexpected intrusions happen to be my specialty." In Kohoutek's current woman's voice there was not a trace of flirtatiousness.

"Excellent," replied Oyermah. "My friend Kohoutek and I were just discussing what's to be done. Unfortunately, there's little I can do to help. Until the two of you make some fundamental decisions, it's possible only to concern oneself with certain details. One such important detail may be the fact that, if my memory serves me correctly, and it most certainly does, in the attic of the old slaughterhouse that used to belong to the late Emilian, may he rest in peace, there is also a rear exit."

Kohoutek had never seen or heard of a secret second entrance to the attic, but he also suddenly felt that it meant little to him.

"That's right," Oyermah continued enthusiastically, "in the other room, not the one with the collection of cardboard boxes you know so well, but the other one, the one in which there's a heap of sawdust in the middle of the floor, while in the corner there's a fossilized pile of hay that remembers Stalinist times."

Kohoutek's current woman blushed for no apparent reason and lowered her head.

"It's right behind that hay, mown while Joseph Vissarionovich was still alive, that you have to look. There ought also to be a hoist with a ship's rope. We used that equipment many a time. Many a time"—a nostalgic note sounded in Oyermah's voice—"many, many a time. Though we didn't sing sailors' shanties but instead worked in utter silence. From the perspective of our last invaders the majority of the operations performed in the late Emilian's old slaughterhouse were illegal and punishable by law. I mean, at certain times for some of our enterprises we could have paid with our heads. And so over the last half century we mastered to perfection the art of the conspiratorial butchering of hogs, the partisan cutting up of the carcass, and the underground production of sausage. At night we would climb the ship's rope into the slaughterhouse, which had been carefully blacked out and as a result was stifling as an inferno; and with the same rope we hauled up the unconscious animals. The snow shone like the heavens, while our shadows bustled about the late Emilian's butcher's establishment, which was supposedly closed down but actually throbbing with life. . . ."

All at once Oyermah broke off, as his seasoned storyteller's instinct told him that the attention of his listeners was distracted. Kohoutek's current woman was still sitting with lowered head; it seemed that her funky little hat would slide off her divine skull at any moment.

She hasn't looked at me once since she arrived, thought Kohoutek. I'm not mistaken: She's decided to take her fate into her own hands.

"Doctor, would you be able to rent me a room?" Kohoutek's current woman asked softly.

Oyermah let out a heavy sigh.

"My dear child," he said, "forgive me, but I can't. I thought about such an eventuality from the start, but I can't."

"No one would come and visit me, not a soul," she whispered convulsively. "I'd take care of the house and cook dinners."

"No," said Oyermah firmly. "It's not a question of whether anyone would come and visit you or not. The fact that a certain story is headed for a particular ending, I just understood myself a moment ago. The reasons are different. Or rather, there's one reason: I'm going to die soon. I don't know if Kohoutek told you, ma'am, that in accordance with local custom this needs to be done before the snows and frosts come. I have maybe another week, maybe only a few days." Oyermah spoke in the cold, dogmatic tone of a person who knows they are uttering an incontrovertible truth. "I don't want you to be here when I'm dying, and I don't want you to be left here alone afterward. My distant relatives would tear you to pieces even before the funeral. That's right, I'm setting off for the next world; I'm fully conscious of it and it's a sufficient reason in itself, so that I don't need to mention arguments of lesser weight, such as for example the spirit of the late Józefina. What would it say, the spirit of my darling Józefina? It wouldn't be happy at all; it might even prey on you at night, ma'am." Oyermah suddenly giggled ominously.

"In that case, Doctor, I have another request," said Kohoutek's current woman.

"Yes?"

"Could I wash my hair in your bathroom?"

"Splendid," replied Oyermah. "In the hall closet you'll find a clean towel, though as far as shampoo is concerned I can only offer calamus-and-hop."

For a good while they sat in silence. When the sound of running water began to come from the bathroom, Oyermah nodded toward the empty glasses. Then they each drank a measure and Oyermah said sententiously, "The idea of gradually improving the attic of the old slaughterhouse and slowly turning it into a proper home collapsed as suddenly as it arose."

"Which doesn't alter the fact that the madness goes on. No normal woman would have come here"—Kohoutek still seemed unable to grasp the fact that his arguments were psychologically simplistic—"and if she did come, after some time for sure, and most definitely after the story was over she would have gone away again. Whereas she is still here."

"Yes, she's still here; you're going away; the world is stood on its head in accordance with the inexorable laws of feminine cruelty. Now where was I?"

"In the room opposite mine . . ."

19

"In the room opposite mine"—Oyermah didn't wait even for a second—"lives a mysterious, suspicious, and repulsive character. A tall, broad-shouldered man of about my height and of indeterminable age. He could be thirty and he could be fifty. Gold-rimmed spectacles. A storm of greasy hair on a tiny nutlike head. Despite the outrageous heat, he always goes about in a tattered autumn overcoat with a hood. Goes about? An overstatement, the wrong word in the wrong place. This person hardly ever leaves his room. Every few days he slips out of his lair for a few minutes, evidently with the goal of doing some shopping—and buying some particularly shabby items, judging by the bundle that he clutches tightly under his arm. I've passed him two or three times in the hallway of the hotel. He doesn't respond to my bow, but just transfixes me with his tiny, piercing, burning eyes. That's right. He doesn't leave his room; but she comes to him every day, and not once, not twice, but several times a day. She is so inconceivably beautiful that she truly seems to be a creature not of this world. For a Japanese she is uncommonly tall. She wears European clothes, always in summer dresses but in dark colors. When she waits outside his door for longer than usual, I can smell the narcotic scent of her body slowly filling my room. The thing is, he doesn't let her in, he refuses to receive her; that is, sometimes he graciously allows her to come in and stay, but this always happens after lengthy negotiations, desperate promises, after she has waited long hours. From the hallway there constantly come the sounds of her futile knocking, tempestuous conversations, his impatient falsetto, her supplicatory whisper. The most dramatic situations take place when he orders her to wait. At these times she simply stands in front of his door. I hear the rustle of her dress; I hear her breathing; I choke on her scent. She sometimes waits several hours for an audience; in such cases she goes downstairs and sits in an armchair in the lobby of the hotel. The situation begins to intrigue me greatly, and so I conduct discreet inquiries among the staff. No one knows anything or is willing to say anything. In the end a shapely chambermaid by the name of Caroline—who, by the way, Kohoutek, did indeed—tells me in absolute confidence that the individual living opposite me is an eminent British essayist who right here, in the Luisendorf guest house, is finishing his book on pre-Raphaelite painting. Who the Japanese woman is and what the connection between them might be, no one knows. Besides, I didn't need to ask about the basic nature of their relationship. Despite the enormous amount of work he has to do, the British essayist has on several occasions allowed his obviously burdensome guest to stay the night.

"The ritual knocking at the door wakes me up one night. I lie in bed and listen. As usual she begs him to let her in; this time, however, her whisper is particularly desperate, she knocks on his door with a special feverishness, and the silence that answers her is all the more disturbing. I get out of bed, put on my dressing gown, and light a cigarette. I look at my watch: It's twenty past two. I pace about my room for half an hour and drink two glasses of whiskey;

during this time, from the hallway I hear her even more dramatic imploring sobs. In the end there is silence. A sudden, staggering silence. I know that neither has she gone away, nor has he let her in. I would have heard. At that time I was a virtuoso of listening; my all-knowing ears knew all about those two. Silence, a hopeless silence. The dark, distant foghorn of a tugboat on the Thames, and then silence once more. A terrible silence presaging some crime. In the end I make my mind up and open the door. The Japanese woman is sitting on the floor, leaning against the wall and sleeping. There are the tracks of drying tears on her divine cheeks.

"It was a sight beyond comprehension and overwhelming in its enchantment. A woman sitting on the floor? Before the war? A Japanese woman? At night in the Luisendorf hotel in London? The era of women sitting on the floor was not to come for years and years! Akiko was at least a quarter of a century ahead of her time. I went up to her and gently touched her arm. She opened her eyes and immediately began to talk. She apologized for the noise and gave some explanation which I didn't understand, since, although she spoke English, it was with the typical, as it were, Samurai accent. Besides, she was crying, she had begun to cry almost at once; she was pointing to the British essayist's door and sobbing like a child once more. When it came down to it, I didn't need to understand what she was saying—I knew the situation through and through. I knocked vigorously on the essayist's door. To my surprise he opened it almost at once. He was wearing a filthy nightshirt; the unbearable stench of manuscripts wafted from his room. He asked me coldly (though, I have to admit, politely) not to disturb his rest; he explained that he was not responsible for the antics of the young Japanese lady, and he was just about to close the door when she literally exploded. She shouted indistinctly, paying no attention to her accent, but this time, Kohoutek, I understood everything, I understood every sentence and every word, and I lapped it up with indescribable delight. She was saying that he was a clown, a bastard, and a hack, that this was categorically the end, that she didn't even despise him or hate him, that she was just utterly indifferent to him.

Like all beautiful women, whom fury releases from the shackles of coquetry, Akiko in her fury was breathtaking. Her raven-black hair, dense and thick as graphite, fell across her forehead; she turned pale, and her dark eyes blazed. A hint of fright, embarrassment, and perhaps a singular smile crossed the essayist's face and slowly, without a word he closed his door. Akiko stood helplessly in the middle of the hallway; while I, allowing myself to be carried along by this extraordinary sequence of events, did something that under normal circumstances I would never have done either before or after: I invited her into my room, to have something to drink and to calm down. And she accepted my offer without a moment's thought.

"Kohoutek, the happiest hours of my life had begun. Within a quarter of an hour we were a pair of good friends who had known each other for years. Within an hour we were planning our life together. Akiko had taken off her sandals; she was sitting in an armchair with her feet tucked under her, drinking whiskey and laughing hysterically at everything I said. Then she taught me Japanese. On a sheet of paper she wrote, or perhaps rather drew, the mysterious Japanese alphabet; she explained what it was in English and told me the Japanese pronunciation. My lord, how zealously, how enthusiastically I repeated each of those curious sounds, so zealously that I remember every one of them to this day. The following morning we were to travel to *hingashi*—the east; our *uchi*—house—was going to stand by the *kawa* or river, in the shadow of a *yama* or mountain; at night, over the roof of our *uchi* the *oki*—moon—would always shine. Her *kokoro*—heart—belonged to me; we were joined by *ai* or love, and our *ai* would be blessed by *kamisama*, God himself. Later I tried to write, or draw; when I made a mistake, she would take me gently by the hand and lead me like a child along the dim trails of the hieroglyphs.

"She said she was hungry. I made her scrambled eggs. It turns out that it's possible to experience the loftiest kind of inner rapture while preparing scrambled eggs. Imagine this scene, Kohoutek: I'm making scrambled eggs over a spirit stove while the beautiful Akiko is standing by me, the whole time resting her hand on my arm as if she were afraid that I'll run away or disappear, and the whole time I keep glancing at her, making sure that she's there and that she exists. And she is there and she exists, because she's wolfing down the scrambled eggs. Then, in a strangely awkward fashion, without taking the spoon out of the cup she drinks tea. The spoon sticking into her cheek and the breadcrumb in the corner of her mouth are irrefutable, necessary, and sufficient proof of her existence. She grows sleepy. She goes into the bathroom while I prepare the bed for her. She comes back. She hangs her thin dress in the wardrobe and embraces me with all her strength. I touch her and all of a sudden I feel a black despair radiating from her like a gust of icy wind. Every sinew of hers, every muscle, her blood, her bones, her heart, everything is permeated with the black rime of despair. Everything the woman does is done out of despair. Every unpredictable step she takes is guided by profound despair. It is out of despair that she storms the door of the odious British essayist (we don't talk about him at all, not a single word is uttered on that topic; when he closed the door to his room he simply ceased to exist), it was out of despair that she had left someone (a husband? a fiancé?— I make guesses from the obscure hints she drops), and it is out of despair that she has found herself in my arms.

"She gets into bed and instantly falls into the abrupt sleep of a child. I sit motionless in the armchair and I'm filled with noble visions and rapturous scenes in which I ease her despair. I stare at her bare, frail arms and I feel that I'm beginning to turn foolish, foolish from happiness. It's growing lighter, and to me it seems as if the golden glow of her skin is filling the room. Akiko wakes up, smiles, and dresses in a particular hurry. We have decided that we'll move out of this guest house as soon as possible, and so now she'll get dressed and go and fetch her things (where? what things? I haven't a clue!), and in the meantime I'll pack and wait for her downstairs in the lobby. She's already dressed and I'm not at all surprised that she leaves virtually without saying goodbye, because after all she'll be back in a moment. I am surprised, however, and mightily at that, by the familiar knocking that is immediately heard in the hallway. This time she doesn't knock for long; a rattle of the lock, the door opens, the door closes, and Akiko disappears forever. Akiko ceases to exist."

Oyermah fell silent for a moment. Kohoutek's current woman had come back from the bathroom; she was standing by the stove, drying and brushing her hair.

"That's right. She ceased to exist," repeated Oyermah, "since then that flighty Japanese woman only ever comes to me in my dreams and whenever I see her it terrifies me, because she's always the bringer of bad tidings. I'm certain that she is dead and has been for a long time. Even then she was barely alive from despair. If she didn't commit suicide soon afterward then she simply perished from her agony. I can't forget her and I'm not able to forgive her. O cruel Akiko." He sighed. "You promised that you'd spend the rest of your life with me, when all you wanted to do was to wait till morning, when the forbidden portal would open up before you. Though who knows, sometimes I think that maybe at that time, as you planned the life we'd share in the *uchi* we'd share, you believed firmly in it all?

"It goes without saying that I left the hotel that day, and London the next; within a week I was back in Poland. Along with portentous dreams of Akiko, I brought back with me a curious mania for giving Anglo-Saxon names to all the local animals. I made it just in time for the outbreak of World War Two. At bottom it could be said that the whole matter ended with a great burst of *uarau*—laughter."

Epilogue

Kohoutek is going away. For how long? Who knows? To Kohoutek it seems that he's going away for good. And as usual he thoroughly believes in his own imaginings. He packs, slips across the lawn that was once the courtyard of the great slaughterhouse, and takes a side street along the river to the railroad station. If someone wrote a book about me, thinks Kohoutek, it could begin as follows: When, in the year of our Lord 1990, Paweł Kohoutek, Doctor of Veterinary Medicine, saw his current woman sitting at the dining room table, he thought he would die. In any case, thinks Kohoutek, I wouldn't survive such a thing; maybe I wouldn't die, but I wouldn't survive it. Die's the last thing I'd do—Kohoutek is all of a sudden overcome by rage—die's the last thing I'd do, one of these days I'm going to believe myself. I wouldn't die—I'd be so scared I'd crap my pants. When in the year of our Lord 1990 Paweł Kohoutek, Doctor of Veterinary Medicine, saw his current woman sitting at the dining room table, he was so scared he crapped his pants. That sounds much better—more rounded and believable. Even she, connoisseur of the literary phrase that she is, would like that sentence. It's another matter whether it's better to crap your pants or to die. It's better to die, because if you die you'll no longer crap your pants, whereas if you crap your pants you'll still die. But best of all is to do what I'm doing: to run away before you crap your pants and before you die. To run away before she sits at the dining room table. To run away before she starts talking with my wife, my child, my mother. To run away before she moves into the room unexpectedly vacated by Miss Wandzia and Miss Wandzia's mother. And so very unexpectedly! From one day to the next and from one hour to the next. For obscure, unexplained, and unaccountable reasons.

Kohoutek missed Miss Wandzia; after all, she belonged to the great company of the female instrumentalists of humanity. The eternal grimace of pain or distaste never left her tiny foxlike face, not even when she was playing Schubert. And now there was silence. As Oyermah put it: a terrible silence presaging some crime. They packed and left in such a hurry that it really did seem as if they had committed a crime or as if someone's hand hungry for vengeance was about to catch up with them at any moment. Once or twice Miss Wandzia was heard weeping; then there would come her odd, nervous yet curiously triumphal laugh. As they said their goodbyes Miss Wandzia's mother cast a watchful and censorious glance at Kohoutek; then they got into a taxicab and were gone. Miss Wandzia's mother, thinks Kohoutek, looked at me as if I were the cause of everything. No, it wasn't me, this time it definitely wasn't me. They were the causes of everything; they left behind an empty room which someone will move into very soon. Kohoutek is certain who it will be, though perhaps he shouldn't be completely, one hundred percent certain. After all, he is not gifted with great intuition. It's unlikely, very unlikely, that he has somehow acquired the intuition of his women. Though it's not inconceivable.

Kohoutek gets on the train. This time, however, he doesn't search for something worthy of notice; he doesn't look patiently into one compartment after another in the hope that his labors will be rewarded. It's still a long time till the departure. For a while Kohoutek sits in his seat, then he goes out into the corridor and opens the window. In front of the old station building Kohoutek's doleful child is standing and staring ahead with unimaginable sadness.

"I must get around to taking him to the zoo," Kohoutek whispers to himself, and feels a strange constriction in his heart, in his throat. "I've promised so many times." And all at once Kohoutek begins calling his child's name and waving his hand; while the child looks about, at first seeming to be afraid, then finally notices Kohoutek and rushes toward him in a child's mad abandon. Kohoutek helps him up the steps, then for a good while is unable to utter a word.

"In the evening we'll call Mommy, and tomorrow we'll go to the zoo," he says at last.

The train moves off. Kohoutek and his child stand at the window and gaze at Kohoutek's hometown, extending across the valley and inhabited exclusively by adherents of the Lutheran faith. The air gradually turns gray, and lights come on in the houses. From up here on the high railroad embankment they can see everything clearly. They can see the church, the parish office, the sports center, and the cemetery on its steep hillside. They can see the old slaughterhouse and the great wooden home in which Dr. Oyermah is dying. In the attic of the old slaughterhouse Oma is standing and looking about helplessly. There's no one there. Oma whispers something soundlessly to herself. In her hands she is holding a yeast babka in wrapping paper. She wanders among the cardboard boxes, limping; she unwraps the paper, eats a tiny piece of babka, waits for some time, for some time looks around in vain, then she hides the babka in one of the boxes and prepares for her laborious return to earth.

In the absolute silence that fills the dark old house, Dr. Oyermah hears the distant rumble of the departing train. He lies inertly on the sofa. He is still wearing the brownish-yellow tweed jacket, black pants, and light blue shirt. All his strength has abandoned him.

Time and again he falls into a sleep deep as the abyss. The somber waters of eternity are rising higher and higher; wave breaks after wave, while his eyelids turn to stone. And before the doctor's eyes there open up all the doors through which he has ever passed. There opens the great iron gate leading to the yard. There open up the doors leading to the hall, to the ice cellar, to the last room in the house. There open the doors to the kitchen, to the storeroom, to the old slaughterhouse. There open the doors to all the stables and cattle sheds which he entered to save the animals or to cut short their suffering. There opens the door to the cellar and the door to the attic. There open the doors to all the bars and inns where he had gathered with friends. There open the doors of homes and the entrances of churches; there open garden wickets and the gates of great courtyards. And Franciszek Józef Oyermah crosses every threshold one more time. There open before him the doors of the hotels in which he has stayed. There opens before him the door of the Luisendorf guest house. There open up before him guest rooms, bedrooms, and dining rooms. Behind the last door, covered in cracked and peeling paint, is a simple sandy path. Oyermah walks up this gently rising track and looks about in astonishment. Is it possible on such an occasion, he thinks, is it possible on such an occasion to be late? Of course not! There she is. She's running toward him in a dark summer dress. She throws her arms around him with all her might. Then she takes him by the hand and leads him toward stupendous landscapes filled with light; she accompanies him to where there are somber waters and dense clouds. But Oyermah is far from feeling a relief lighter than air; he continues to sense his agonizing solitude and the pain in every last corner of his body. And he suddenly realizes that he has no desire to part either with his solitude or with his pain. And he stands in the middle of the path and pulls his hand from Akiko's hand, which is all of a sudden gripping his with unparalleled strength, and he says angrily, "Thank you very much, my dear Akiko, but now I don't have the slightest desire. You should have given yourself to me in thirty-nine or at the very least not gone crawling right back to that joker's room. What

130

do you think," he shouts, "that I'll spend the whole of eternity wandering around in your pagan afterworld? Out of the question!" And before Akiko can assume a hurt expression she vanishes, as do the sandy path and the stupendous landscapes filled with light. Oyermah wakes up and looks at the blue stove, the piano, the reproduction of *The Last Supper* hanging on the wall. He feels like someone who has come through a serious illness, weakened yet strangely restored and purified. He gets up from the sofa and walks to the window. It's a frosty morning of another day. The air is bright. Everything is covered by a thick coating of snow that has fallen in the night. On the hillside opposite, a figure can be seen. High up, where human habitations end, someone is toiling across the white expanse, heading toward the fir woods. Oyermah strains his eyes and is certain he can see a funky little hat, a backpack on narrow shoulders, and a colossal suitcase leaving indecipherable marks in the snow.